Immigration: The Contest
Bad News from The Island

Carlos Gámez Pérez

Translated by Arthur M. Dixon

I0557733

Immigration: The Contest
(Bad News from The Island)
BY CARLOS GÁMEZ
FIRST EDITION 2019
ORIGINAL TITLE: MALAS NOTICIAS DESDE LA ISLA

TRANSLATION FROM SPANISH ARTHUR M. DIXON

Published by **Katakana editores** All rights reserved © 2019

EDITOR: Omar Villasana
DESIGN: Elisa Orozco
COVER ART: Joaquín González

KATAKANA EDITORES CORP.
Weston FL 33331
✉ katakanaeditores@gmail.com

CARLOS GÁMEZ PÉREZ

Translated from the Spanish
by Arthur M. Dixon

Immigration: The Contest
Bad News from The Island

katakana
editores

For Gema Pérez, for all she taught me,
and for Cristina and Gabriel, for everything else.

Explanatory Note

According to the dictionary of the Royal Spanish Academy, the words "immigrate" (*inmigrar*) and "emigrate" (*emigrar*) and their various derivations (emigrant, emigration, immigrant, immigration) are very similar. For the word "emigrate," we find the following definitions: "Said of a person, a family, or a people: To leave or abandon one's own country with the aim of settling in another, foreign country. || To temporarily be absent from one's own country in order to undertake certain tasks in another. || To abandon one's usual residence within one's own country in search of a better livelihood." For the word "immigrate," on the other hand, we find the definition: "Said of a native of a country: To arrive in another in order to settle in it, especially with the intention of forming new colonies or of taking up residence in previously formed colonies," which contains hints of ghettos and invasion. The term "migration," for its part, is reserved for historical exoduses. These distinct meanings for related words, as well as the fact that some people consider the foreigner an immigrant while the native always retains the category of emigrant, have greatly conditioned their use in this text.

"Long he wandered over land and sea,
dragged on by the will of the gods."

VIRGIL
Aeneid

I'm afraid the news from The Island isn't good, as I shall relate. I shall do so in this virtual space, open to the whole world. This is my effort to recount what I believe is the true story of *Immigration: The Contest*, including the deaths: the terrible accident that has left the audience shaken to its core. If I were the affected person, which I'm not, I would say this story serves as an homage to the victims. It's a far sight from the tear-jerking program the production company just put out; a special that aired, in sensationalist fashion, a series of shots of the bodies floating in the sea as well as a retransmission of the news segments showing the accident's impact on the victims' families. All presented by a professional who was hired with one clear objective in mind: to help the pain reach the other side of the screen through recurring soundbites and platitudes, well known for their efficacy in mass media. You already know the ending: the images of the state funeral and the final verdict.

This way of telling a story is far from ideal; it's cowardly, like when you watch from a balcony as they murder a foreigner in an uninhabited city, even if the only reason you keep quiet and watch is out of fear they'll kill you too. But we are already used to the fact that, in audiovisual media, there can be no interaction with the receiver. This has allowed for the distortion of the true reasons behind the final challenge in my sector, which was not in the script and ended in tragedy, as well as the censorship of the images of the accident that were inappropriate for broadcast; reasons and images I know all too well.

11

It's curious. After so many years working in the audiovisual sector, now I wouldn't be able to tell this story on the screen, partially out of fear of the control exercised by Silvio Pérez and his assistant, producer Vladimir Lazarovich. What else could you expect from a couple of guys who feel obliged to micromanage every detail of their projects, just like in the interviews, scripts, step outlines, and scenes they wrote for their all-powerful production company's reality shows? I was always hoping to receive their approval in order to make my voice heard, like a latter-day Sheherezade. Nevertheless, they will have no say over the blog I'm starting today. On the Internet, one owns one's own work. Here, you can converse with me directly. You can send me an email at verdaderahistoriadeinmigracion@gmail.com if you like, although, due to the high volume of data I receive, more than a few bits of information may pass by unnoticed; the same thing probably happens with my own web presence, just another drop in the ocean of data. There are already thousands of pages published about the accident, even though the events took place so recently, and some are full of nonsense. It won't matter much that I was a member of the production team, in charge of the edition where everything happened, nor that I was a first-hand witness of the events; nor that, to some extent, I was a participant in the tragedy. But the feeling of guilt that this imposes upon me—as well as the fact that yesterday I was unable to tell my ex-girlfriend, Ingrid, about what happened—are circumstances that cause me a pain that was only exacerbated when I watched Silvio Pérez's special tonight.

I've been watching the contestants' final confessionals, which took place just before the accident. I watched them in the production control room of The Island, now deserted, from which we could observe everything that happened in the sea thanks to the "Eye of Europe." I have matched the images to my previous transcriptions of their statements, and I have tried to understand to the letter the words pronounced by the living as well as the dead. If I had the emission rights,

12

I would upload the images to this space so you could judge for yourselves, but they belong to the show's producer, and Silvio Pérez would block the page and file a lawsuit against me. So, for the next few nights, I'm going to write down each one of their testimonies. I've had to substitute the visual experience for the literary media best adapted to the contestants' confessionals, even though I know these are no longer their voices, but rather the memory their voices have left in me. I cannot reproduce their voices, the translation is impossible. Even watching them again, I can't bring them back; not I nor anyone else because the victims are—or were—their exclusive owners. And so, my voice is the only one you will find here. We could say this is fiction: the fiction that arises as I write my impressions of the final statements of each of the participants in my sector. I'll start with the Kid. 田

Name: the Kid

Age: 17

Skin color: brown

Eye color: dark brown

Hair color: black

Profession: tour guide

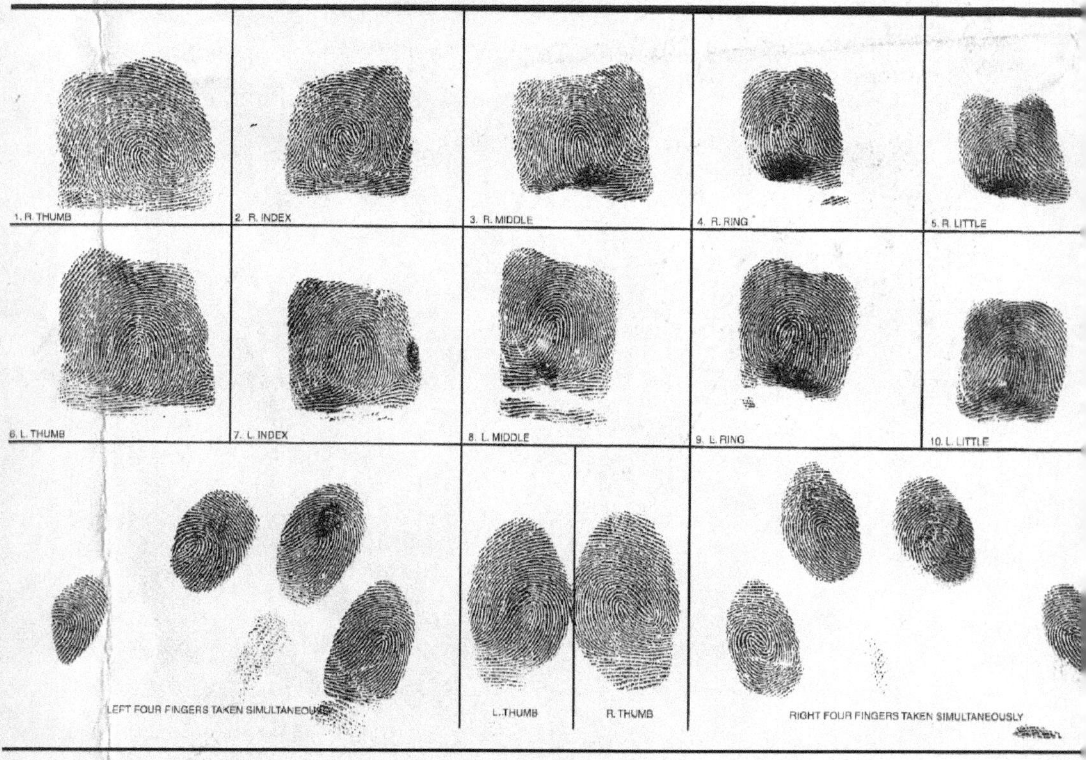

1. R. THUMB	2. R. INDEX	3. R. MIDDLE	4. R. RING	5. R. LITTLE
6. L. THUMB	7. L. INDEX	8. L. MIDDLE	9. L. RING	10. L. LITTLE

LEFT FOUR FINGERS TAKEN SIMULTANEOUSLY	L. THUMB	R. THUMB	RIGHT FOUR FINGERS TAKEN SIMULTANEOUSLY

Sign--

The Kid

I'M THE KID, that's what everyone calls me; it's not to show off, that's what they called me where I come from and that's what my companions have called me since I made it onto The Island, and the audience adopted it immediately as my nickname. I want to start my last confessional by thanking the audience for their support; a name like the Kid always implies a show of affection, shows of affection like the one bestowed upon me by the expat Spanish writer before I came here; he called me the same thing: the Kid. I entered this contest so I could see him again.

I was born in the city formerly known as Fez; but I grew up in the slums of what was once called Tétouan; I was sadly happy there until I met him and realized I was missing something. I often stopped by the transport station to make myself a few numeraries as a tour guide, or an errand boy, or a shoe shiner; whatever was needed. It was in the transport waiting room where I came across the expat Spanish writer: grotesquely attractive, with that Castilian diction he would later teach me; I approached him and, with what poorly spoken Spanish I had back then, I asked him if he needed help; I do, kid, I remember he said. Later he would call me his "Little Red Riding Hood," but that's another story; that day he settled for "kid." The point is that he asked me to join him on his journey through the streets of the city that was once called Tétouan; I agreed with gusto in exchange for some numeraries.

If my memory doesn't fail me, because these recollections are now fragmented, I think we strolled that day through the emblem-

15

atic neighborhoods of Tétouan; we followed a path that now strikes me as a circuit, from the periphery to the center. We visited Bled, the plaza of Sayyida al-Hurra; we took Tranqat street; we crossed in front of the building of The Union and the Phoenix and reached the gardens of Riad al-Ochak; there we sat on a bench and he, tactlessly penetrating the membrane of my trust, adulated me again and again; it was like a whip, his language was inaccessible and enveloping, but with a crack he would stretch out and his compliments would become sweetly stabbing, like a bee's sting, I don't know how to explain it. He told me I had just conquered his heart and I would always reign in the most intimate depths of his being; then he branded me a virginal, perfect creature and, after caressing my face, he invited me to go and visit him in Tangier; he gave me his card, which included his email address:

escritorespañolexpatriado@gmail.com.

While I accompanied him back to the transport station, I lost hold of myself. I still treasure in my memory, like a precious elixir, that kiss on the cheek with which he inoculated me with his breath and said goodbye. After that, he would respond hastily to my first emails, which I wrote from an Internet booth close to my family's house; in those messages, he adulated me again; I still keep them in my inbox, consulting them from time to time in sadness to give myself a shot of good spirits. It was predictable that, although I was a good Muslim, when I turned sixteen I would decide to run away in search of him; the option presented itself as the only alternative to the poverty that surrounded me. I escaped from my home to live close to him; I was just a boy; now I'm the Kid.

That was how I came to Tangier; images I recall at this moment, although I know they are fragments that only pool together as I speak them: the sun at the top of the sky; the music played on a flute; the coins of the golden-haired European tourists with their devices at the ready: video cameras, tablets, iPhones; the Sons and

Daughters of the French Revolution before the facade of the old, dilapidated Grand Socco, beside the newly opened shopping malls; and after that, the alley by the old synagogue, in ruins, next to the artisanal whips made of Moroccan leather displayed on the wall, near the new neighborhood of brothels where the young soldiers on leave strolled by—their dark, menacing dicks hanging between their legs, like a battering ram waiting to punch a hole through the back cavern. Then the memory of the path toward the Moorish café where, months later, I would captivate the Spanish writer with my dance of womanly undulations, although that was something I still didn't know as I looked over the café's terrace; no, that day I just saw the smattering of old queens who had returned to the city after the end of the war, sitting on the balcony, watching out for adolescents like me who were about to open up to life, subtle invaders of their intimacy; all so shameless: Sexy, lovely, calling me kid again; that threw me off balance, the memory of the expat Spanish writer returned and, suddenly, I met the eager gaze of the Scandinavian; I would meet him soon, the Spanish writer introduced us days later; the Scandinavian told me he was a *connoisseur* for whom Africa held no more secrets; but I felt his gaze penetrate my body in search of the resounding secrets that must have resisted him on other occasions; I don't know how to explain it.

The Moorish café was the place where the Spanish writer claimed to have found "young men with copper skin and white teeth, with little, wandering, affectionate souls: normally with no education or employment: but open and understanding," young men to whom he also introduced me; he did so while I lived in the aristocratic mansion that served as the scene of my first true encounter with him, at whose doors I arrived with delight that morning I still treasure in my memory. I remember the route from the Moorish café that I had reviewed online until I could remember all the instructions: get to the covered gallery: contemplate the decrepit foosball tables that go unmentioned on Google Maps: advance around the wall in front of Hotel Cuba: continue down Ben Charki: walk by the alleyway with a solid wooden door: and then the rooftop café: turn right down Tapiro: pass in front of Les Aliments Sherezade: and come face to face with your fate: the luxurious mansion where, from this moment on, you would live.

I stayed there for awhile, just a few months; but one day the Spanish writer decided to stop being an expat of the country that was once called Spain and that now forms part of the newly re-established European Union; an entity that was abstract until it started controlling the flow of people across its borders; an entity that, as if overnight, surrounded itself with walls. At that time, when the Spanish writer left, they kicked me out of the luxurious mansion with its couches and rugs; I had to scrape up a living from the streets of Tangier; and I started hanging around with those young men with copper skin and white teeth —my rivals before, my comrades from that moment on— who were already starting to wither from the glue they inhaled and the drugs they consumed; young men with little, wandering souls, much like the jobs with which they fed themselves, almost all related to prostitution, whether with the local smattering of old queens or with the other foreign gays who lived in the city: a few numeraries in exchange for an invasion of foreign fluids into the body.

My life was like theirs until I found out about the contest and decided to show up to the qualifying challenge. As you all know, in our area the challenge involves crossing the fence, a fence six meters tall that surrounds all the contestant admission centers in North Africa.

It was a failure; it was tricky to scale the rope due to the anti-climbing mesh they had installed; and to avoid the mechanical dogs, which bit at our ankles just to make things more difficult. The weakest youngsters slid down to the ground and took

18

off running from the dogs; excellent, shouted the organizers, and they applauded to give the scene some atmosphere. I got up to the top with little effort, thanks to the womanly undulations that had captivated the Spanish writer; nevertheless, I didn't anticipate the razor wire that awaited me at the highest point, cutting away at my delicate hands and dancer's arms; and my bones crunched against the ground, next to the fence but on the wrong side, while I watched a few imposing Sub-Saharans —strapping, as the expat Spanish writer called them— who, tipped off by some friend about the contest's new rules this season, wore work gloves that were barely even scratched as they jumped the fence; as the organizers said days later, those blades served to make the challenge more selective and to ensure that only the most physically gifted reached the second phase: only the ones the Europeans needed most.

There, at the challenge, I saw Mamadou for the first time; he was one of those Sub-Saharans; he did pass the preliminary phase; I only received the appropriate pats on the back, down on the ground, along with a false smile from one of the organization's members; a woman with blonde hair and terribly smeared lipstick who said to me with a foreign accent: Well done, thanks for participating. You're young. Try again next year. Best of luck. It seemed like she was in charge of the whole thing; later I would discover that she was the Minister; she must have mentioned my youth because there were no children this time; compelled by desperation, some parents had signed up their young children in previous seasons and thrown them over the fence, leaving them severely wounded, until the organization banned minors under the age of sixteen from competing and placed cameras and control towers on the fences; that's why I'm the Kid this season, just like I was for the Spanish writer while he was living as an expat in Tangier; nobody younger than me can compete here.

19

It took weeks for my wounds from the razor wire to heal; I must admit that at first I promised myself I would never participate again; if I couldn't get past the initial selection, how would I survive the later challenges? So I settled for taking long walks, looping around Tangier until I was standing before the sea; there, I would look out at the Strait along with my new co-adventurers: the young men with copper skin and white teeth, with little, wandering, souls. I looked at the unsettled waters, the rafts, the infected, open wound, and behind it The Big Fence, the membrane that separated me from the fate I longed for on the other shore, and from the expat Spanish writer, whom I was beginning to forget.

Then he appeared on cable television; it was on a show about books on the Art channel that I had discovered during those months that were, for me, a first and passionate immersion in the world of culture. Now I tuned in from an Internet booth with pirated Netflix, to learn more so he would feel shamefully proud of me if we met again; the expat Spanish writer always said, and I'm quoting verbatim, that I should boast about my culture, about the music of my land, which was popular yet elevated; but I didn't see it like that, I wanted to treasure the knowledge he possessed, and I thought that was only possible through accumulating the greatest possible awareness of that other elevated knowledge: his own. There, on the television program, I saw him speaking that complex, rich Spanish he taught me, riddled with Mozarabic loan words; like my own, although I used them unconsciously while he did so consciously, combining Arabic and Berber terms with those of a Haketia that no longer exists and that I would have liked to learn; but that's another story.

While I watched him through the screen, I entered a state of sad ecstasy; once again, my body was invaded by the strange influence of Little Red Riding Hood; I forgot his departure and other dark elements of our separation that still rattled painfully within me, and

20

the alchemy that the sight of him produced within me served as an incentive to stop being a hostage of my own fate. A frantic impulse to participate in the contest drove me to try again.

It happened on my next walk, as I roamed along with eleven of those young men with copper skin and white teeth; I don't know how to explain it; instead of looking again at the seductive and dangerous Strait, I set my sights on the abandoned dinghy beside the dock around which the waves churned, and on the opening that had been revealed after the recent storm in the section of fence outside the contestant admission center that bordered on the sea; it must have been a stroke of luck, a gift from Allah; I didn't think twice and, in the blink of an eye, I had jumped onto the boat, passed through the hole in the fence, and beaten the contest's first challenge, albeit in an unorthodox fashion, together with Nadir, one of those young men with copper skin and white teeth, who accompanied me on my attempt.

We spent a while there, in the contestant admission center; forty days to be exact, with very little space because the turnout was tremendous this year. We exercised on the adjoining patio, since the center was originally planning to organize more challenges in order to choose the contestants, but in the end they changed the script and decided to make the cut according to age. I'm the Kid, it was obvious that they were going to pick me by that criterion. At the dock I saw a few familiar faces, like Mamadou's; inexplicably, Nadir stayed on land. I asked one of the organizers and he told me it was a programming issue; they had been observing us through the cameras with which they controlled the whole facility; apparently, the audience reaction had given them cause to leave Nadir in the center even though he was young. For the expat Spanish writer, he would have been one of those young men with copper skin and white teeth, with a little, wandering soul, but the organizers saw him only as a physically gifted youngster. The problem is that, ac-

21

cording to the organizer, the program coordinators saw him differently: they saw him as an alpha male, and that was a profile that tended to intimidate the audience. So, in spite of his notable physical aptitude for the job, they had decided to eliminate him.

I sighed, thanking Allah for the womanly undulations that so captivated the expat Spanish writer and that, I thought, had won me the favor of the program coordinators; I did so while we boarded a few long ferries and one of the members of the organization who had accompanied us to the pier said: They're conditioned for the journey; but I looked at how the bodies were crammed into the boat and I didn't understand what this conditioning could mean, until the man, in response to complaints from some of the passengers, said: Don't spoil the fun. The challenges that await you at the end of the trip will be harder than this, you should think positive; he said all of this in front of one of the cameras that transmitted live, and then I understood not only the language he had used but also its crux.

The vessel set off into the sea; at the beginning of the journey, the passengers were in a good mood; we were the chosen ones and that raised our spirits; hymns were sung and cries of joy were heard; but, before long, the heat grew intense and many of us started complaining of thirst, and the waves seemed so high that the weak started crying and the religious started praying, myself included, although I recognize that I was calm because behind the words spoken on the dock I had sensed the *baraka*; I don't know how to explain it, it must come down to Allah; for some strange reason, I knew this was a hidden filter in the game; I was completely sure that there were hidden cameras in some part of the canoe and they were putting us through a surprise challenge in difficult conditions, as they had in previous seasons.

I decided not to fall into the trap and I concentrated. I thought about things that really mattered to me. I tried to remember the confusing teachings I had received from the Spanish writer, his lessons on Spanish language, taught as if it were a natural science; the stroll to the Moorish café every evening, always following the same path, the same one I walked my first day in Tangiers but backwards: pass in front of Les Aliments Sherezade: turn left up Tapiro: walk by the rooftop café: and then the alleyway with a solid wooden door: continue up Ben Charki: advance around the wall in front of Hotel Cuba: get to the covered gallery: contemplate the decrepit foosball tables that go unmentioned on Google Maps: and come face to face with your fate: the facade of the Moorish café: and inside the daily conversation between the Spanish writer and the Scandinavian: then he introduced you: and you felt the sting of his gaze unfurl and then lasciviously penetrate your body: even though you had not yet captivated him with your dance of womanly undulations.

In those days, the first of our relationship, the Spanish writer limited himself to teaching me to speak his language, and I learned about a culture we thought we shared at some open table in the back of the café; back then, he always told me a version of the story of Little Red Riding Hood in which she was a boy; a virginal, perfect little boy who didn't have to go help his grandmother, but rather a high-ranking gentleman called Rodrigo who was very far away, in a luxurious palace that could only be accessed by climbing a staircase made of shells; this Little Red Riding Hood didn't have to bring Sir Rodrigo cakes or butter or honey, as in the usual story; what he had to do was get inside Rodrigo's bedroom and cure him of an infectious disease using a pin. Rodrigo, who belonged to the highest echelon of the Spanish nobility, had contracted this disease in the most lustful phase of his life, and he needed Little Red and the pin to survive and avoid the people's rumors; for that reason, he looked at the boy with ever deeper eyes and ever longer teeth, day after day; until, one morning, Little Red asked

23

Rodrigo the questions everyone knows, which were followed by Rodrigo's responses, which are not necessary to repeat here except for the last one, when he shouted: the better to eat you with, and he jumped on Little Red, covering him with all of his adult's body; then, with a single pinpoint movement, he penetrated the domains of his cavern, flooding into veins, arteries, and all the space the opening would allow, which the expat Spanish writer strangely referred to as The Cava; that was the part of the story I never understood, even though I understood I was listening to the story of a boy with a life similar to mine, if we weren't indeed the very same person. Nor did I understand what he was saying about the Little Red boy, about a sweet whip, and about the violation of the sacred cavern, although I would later discover it was an African legend that had been distorted in what was once called Spain and had thereby reached the Spanish writer, in the same way that, in Africa, the story of Little Red Riding Hood was distorted, but that's another story.

The truth is that in those legends the innocent always seems guilty, and the Spanish writer's story was no different; he presented Rodrigo as the powerful master of the palace, and the little boy had no business resisting a domination he couldn't even understand; that feeling of guilt was accented when a relative of Little Red appeared, Julián or Urbano or Ulyan—now my memory is blurred—to save him from certain castration and take him back to his own people after slicing open Rodrigo's belly with a knife.

On the boat, surrounded by sobs to which I had grown immune, I remembered that, when the Spanish writer finished his story, I would feel again the sensation of listening to the tale of a boy who had been hoping to run into me to tell me about his life and hear about mine, and to discover that they had been almost identical, although, unlike Little Red, I was just the second of seven brothers, and I knew my family from the city that was once called Tétouan

24

was not going to reclaim me because they were too busy looking for work for the firstborn and feeding the other five to worry about the escapades of the second son in Tangier with an expat Spanish writer.

Immersed in these thoughts, I spotted the lights of the port of The Island; that was where the final phase of the Spanish-language edition of the contest would take place. It was located halfway across the sought-after Strait; at that moment, from other boats, some men with megaphones informed us that the entire journey had been filmed and the audience had decided that some contestants were not worthy of passing to the next phase, and I gave thanks to Allah and felt proud for having detected the hidden challenge; two members of the organization came aboard our boat and started handing out life-jackets with an emblem reading *Immigration*; they came in two colors: some had numbers on them and others didn't. Then they read aloud the names of those who had been eliminated and gave them orange life-jackets. Again, I was among those selected and I received a flourescent green life-jacket with well-marked digits; mine was a number seven. They moved us all onto a larger vessel, where we were received by people in uniforms who gave us water, food, and thermal blankets. Then they registered us and took our personal belongings; it seemed more like a floating customs office than one of the contest organization's boats, I don't know how to explain it. After that, they grouped us according to the color of our vests and made us sit down on a crate before sending us to be interviewed. I remember, during the wait, we ate eggplant and I smiled remembering the amusing words of the Spanish writer about a chronicler called Cide Hamete Benengeli, whose last name sounded like "eggplant" in Spanish, so he called him *berenjena*. Then it was my turn to be questioned, and they wanted to know my motivations to compete while they took my photo and fingerprints. Finally, they divided us up by editions.

Those of us who were assigned the Spanish sector were led to another boat and moved to The Island; there they took us to a courtyard and made us take our clothes off; we found ourselves beside participants from other places; there were eight of us in total, with just one woman: Amina, who took her clothes off far from the group for modesty's sake. She says she remembers me from before; but I don't think I met her until that moment. Once we were all arrayed in a perfect line, just how the Europeans like it, they turned on hoses placed on the roofs of the buildings that surrounded the courtyard; this ritual was repeated every morning from then on; they said they saved money that way and kept us clean, but the pressure of the hoses was so high that four contestants from our sector protested to the program's directors. The next day they were eliminated.

From then on we acted even more prudently, because we had reason to think there would be new last-minute discards and other sorts of surprises, like the first challenge in our new destination. It consisted of giving a confessional to the audience about our opinion of the newly re-established European Union, the society that was going to take in the winner; at the same time, we had to show off our oratory skills. Later I would discover that this was the initial challenge in every season of *Immigration*, after the the leaders of the newly re-established Union complained about the migrants' ignorance of European culture; but at first, since none of us knew anyone who had gotten so far in the contest, we were all taken aback by the news. There were protests among the other participants; they didn't understand why, since the selection had been based on physical aptitude up to that moment, in preparation for future labor, the organizers would decide on a more intellectual challenge; what's more, we didn't yet know what a confessional was, I don't know how to explain it. Nonetheless, I knew the odds were in my favor thanks to my having studied the language with the expat Spanish writer and the fondness for culture I have felt since then, although it was evident that there would be more challenges in repayment for the virulence of our complaints. Mamadou was one of those who protested most; he stuck to the argument that what the newly re-established European Union needed most was muscle; and in short order he had showed his biceps to the camera on multiple occasions. He wouldn't take long to confront me when, weeks later, during one of the specials, he discovered the true content of my first confessional. Until then, it had been secret, like those of the others, but the organizers decided to make a few fragments public; that day, the day of the special, Mamadou got in my face; he told the audience they should think of me as the "decadent" contestant who was favored by this type of challenge; his words reminded me of Amina. He assured them that, in his country, homosexuality did not exist, that they wiped it out with a stroke of the machete; people like Mamadou tend to feel very insecure around homosexuals, they think that when we admire their muscles we're hoping to take them to bed; their linear mentality allows for no other alternative; they don't conceive of all the possible curvilinear shapes of human relationships. For them, suffering the woes of being a migrant is enough to feel superior to those who suffer further marginalizations; and they always argue that homosexuality is a sign of depravation, as if I didn't know queers from their own countries, I can spot them from a mile away; I told them so. That dispute, which was the zenith of a rivalry that had been growing throughout the weeks we lived together, polarized the audience.

The point is that I've only had one friend here: the girl from the French edition. Because since the day I came to The Island I've suffered all sorts of attacks, such as the needles I found every morning in my bed, in our dormitory full of bunks, which disturbed my already light sleep; even worse were the insults and threats that

27

one day appeared on the mirror above the sinks: FAGGOT KID, written in my used-up lipstick, along with the nail polish they had stolen from me the night before splattered over the basin and my broken eyeliner pencil, adding insult to injury, even though I kept all my things under lock and key, and so I had to start defending myself; Allah forgive me, but when they weren't looking I would go into the locker room, where there are no cameras in order to respect our intimacy, use a lock pick to open Mamadou's, and cut holes in the underwear through which his chosen one's manhood emerged, because I thought he was the only one who could be writing those denigrating messages, given Amina's bad Spanish and the fact that Cissé had already left, and I amused myself imagining the head of Mamadou's penis sticking out of his underpants like a black battering ram; of course, he didn't get the joke; he certainly suspected me, and it didn't take much for him to get angry whenever we had to work together; but he never found out.

I suppose my enmity with Mamadou and Amina was the reason behind the poisoning. I could swear it was provoked, that my training in the labyrinthine streets of Tangier along with the young men with copper skin and white teeth turned me into someone who never got sick, as little as I was, as was demonstrated in my remarkable performance in the hot bed challenge, and as was not demonstrated in the greenhouse challenge because I felt too weak to compete against Mamadou and his urge to go above and beyond, even though I was used to working in the fields since I was a boy. The fact of the matter is, I think the poisoning took place after my first confessional went public; it must have been either then or just after, when we went through the police checkpoint challenge, which I passed with no problems despite Amina's rudeness because I was used to being harassed by the Tangier police, always looking to take advantage of us. After the challenge, we ate rice with olives, carrots, and artichoke seasoned with lime for

28

lunch; perhaps one of my co-competitors, maybe Mamadou, who preferred not to eat a bite, slipped something toxic into my food, because at that very moment I started to feel the stomach pains, the tingling sensation, the irritation, and finally the hallucinations in the contest's infirmary. In those hallucinations, I found myself with Little Red climbing up the shell staircase of Rodrigo's palace, and he gave me his pin and compelled me to live a life identical to his own; I also dreamed I was walking toward the confessional room and, in perfect Spanish, I recited my first statement to the audience, which was nothing but what I had learned in the expat Spanish writer's classes and what I had later discovered for myself; I don't know how to explain it: that the Spaniards had been the attack dogs of the true colonizers of Africa: the French and the English; how could the supposedly civilizing mission attributed to colonialism be completed by a country that's incapable of civilizing itself, a society that, back then, had the same type of savage attitudes and behaviors in its territory as those it claimed to combat in African lands; only the furthest-right military men, a gang of uncultured despots, believed all that stuff about Spanish colonization of North Africa. The point is that the inhabitants of both sides of the Strait have acted with the same cruelty, we have suffered the same quarrels and divisions, we have hated each other with the same passion with which we hate our brothers, we have been essentially the same; the only difference has been the masters who employed us.

As you all well know, what I just said, which is what I think, was not what I said in my first confessional; I only dreamed the words I just spoke beside Little Red on the shell staircase; I would imagine I was talking to the audience, but then I would wake up with a start in the contest's infirmary, frightened, imagining that the cameras had recorded everything and they were going to eliminate me. I remember those days with true terror.

Luckily, the hallucinations were just an effect of the medications prescribed to fight off the poisoning; a compromising word never left my lips, Allah protected me. Little by little, I got back on my feet. My poisoning, far from turning the audience against me, had gotten them on my side, and so the dirty trick played by whoever decided to poison me—I assumed it was Mamadou, the same one who had written those messages on the bathroom mirror, although I have no proof—hadn't worked out; what's more, for the day of the real confessional, I had composed a speech that I knew would meet with the viewers' approval: I had stressed my condition as a homosexual and the fact that I was a minor, and I had done so in the perfect Spanish that the expat Spanish writer had taught me: a language riddled with words that were originally from Arabic, but that the audience of the Spanish-language edition was unable to distinguish from their own linguistic substrate; and in this way, I put things clearly: only in Europe would my rights be respected, even though that was a lie, even though the audience had no idea how gays were treated in cultures like mine, even though they were completely ignorant of the reality of homosexuals outside the western world.

Europeans love to feel like the saviors, to believe human rights are defended thanks to their culture, as if homosexuals hadn't been persecuted and insulted in past eras in Europe, while Muslims told queer stories like the ones in the *One Thousand and One Nights*, like that of Mahmud-el-Bilateral or the inclinations of Abu Nowas, or love affairs of a markedly lesbian nature that westerners seemed unaware of; but they carry this paternalist vision of the world in their blood; the expat Spanish writer had told me so, and I had to take advantage of it; and so I continued to show off according to all the prejudices associated with my ethnicity, which I repudiated publicly while knowing they were common to the majority of viewers: machismo, the backwardness of our society,

30

the negative influence of religion although I am a true believer; talking points that are foreign neither to Europe nor to their newly re-established Union, but that work wonders if you want to make yourself pass as a migrant who's going to integrate perfectly into the receiving society because you even share its prejudices; so the next move had to be a strong enumeration of critiques against other migrant groups represented in the contest: critiques of radical Muslims like Amina, critiques of Sub-Saharans, who seemingly always left a woman behind in Africa and who smell so different, not to mention their skin tone; judgments that coincide precisely with the Spanish public's perception of these groups, and that tried to exonerate European society for its racism; besides creating the impression of sharing prejudices with the audience, my words gave off the idea that the whole world is racist, not just Europeans; and my strategy worked, at least with the audience of the Spanish-language edition, which was in charge of choosing our finalist, and so I ended up turning the audience in my favor and received a magnificent score; although this also led to my problems living with Mamadou and Amina, who, when they were shown the most controversial passages of my confessional, didn't understand that what they were hearing wasn't what I thought, but rather what I needed to say in order to accumulate a good number of points and end up winning the contest, if that makes sense.

But no, this is my last confessional, my last speech; although fortune has been on my side through these lies, now I must tell the truth, even if it keeps me from winning; but I know that if I triumph I will manage to make my way back to the expat Spanish writer, and I couldn't lie to him even though he was the one who provoked the first invasion after the beautiful dance of womanly undulations that I put on for him to the rhythm of the drums in the Moorish café; from the look in his eyes I knew I had lit his inner flame; then, jealous of the look in the Scandinavian's eyes after my dance, he laid down his kief pipe and grabbed me by the wrist so hard it hurt and dragged me down the looping path we walked every day to get home, which was the same path I walked down on my first day in Tangier, that is: go running from the Moorish café and get to the covered gallery although neither your urgency nor the decrepit foosball tables appear in the instructions on Google maps: advance around the wall in front of Hotel Cuba: continue down Ben Charki, walk by the alleyway with a solid wooden door: and then the rooftop café: turn right down Tapiro: and pass in front of Les Aliments Sherezade until you come face to face with your fate: the luxurious mansion of the expat Spanish writer: there, feel the pain in your wrist that he has not yet released: walk through the hallway: climb the shell staircase up to his bedroom, pushed along by his orders: watch how he takes his clothes off: look at the stinger of his battering ram: his white whip: and then the black, spiral-shaped whip that remains fixed on the wall: the indispensable prolongation of the expat Spanish writer: now in the bed: then he attracts you with unmoving violence: he seems to want to break your delicate body: he even makes you kneel: beg for forgiveness: you do so while the spiral cord unrolls: he crosses your back with three lashes: scars that have disappeared but that keep hurting you from the inside: ... : then he takes you by the shoulders: he turns your body on the bed: he penetrates you: at first with a certain tact: Am I hurting you?: but minutes later without mercy: uncontrolled in his lust: riding, riding you with his extended stinger: with his white whip that knows the unknown path to your guts: taking no notice of your cries of pain into the pillow: of your tears: of your complaints of suffering: of your begging him to stop: because you're still a kid: and your narrow cavern is not yet ready for his handiwork: but he is at his peak: blinded by his revelry: ready to inject the liquid: to invade your

32

essence: and he shouts those words again and again: DRIVE YOUR KID WITH THE LASH OF A WHIP: then you understand everything about the sacred cave: and that the story of your life is really a variation on the story of Little Red Riding Hood: he and you become one at that precise instant: and you discover your life is identical to his.

That was how my passion became a burning iceberg. That night the pain in my bones was unbearable; it only got worse in the following days; and I couldn't get to sleep because, after the invasion, the expat Spanish writer started flirting with other boys, those young men with copper skin and white teeth, with little, wandering, affectionate souls, whom he had told me about and who ended up becoming my comrades. Every time he walked into the high-class, luxurious mansion with a new companion, I felt a sting of jealousy, just like the sting I had received from the whip of the Spanish writer, whose favors had been denied me for weeks; until, one day, he left. I thought he left in search of another kid in another palace or another luxurious mansion. Now I know that he left because he was none other than Little Red himself, the little boy from the story he had told me so many times, but with another name: Alvarito. That's why we had to come apart: he had initiated me such that I could have an existence identical to his own, and two equal images cannot live together. Since then, I have only seen him again on cable television; that's why I'm here, trying to win the contest and have some sort of future once I find him again, to try to take the place of the last kid who took the place of the kid who took the place of Little Red in a world without a future; because I'm the Kid. 🁢

33

The first time I heard the Kid's confessional, in the controversial Final Special, it made me angry. I had believed his words from the first challenge, believed in a certain international standard of homosexuality that could only be located in the West. Curiously, the Minister of Integration of the newly re-established European Union thought the same thing, even though she was homophobic. I know because we both formed part of the jury that decided who should pass to the final phase of the contest. We discussed the subject together.

In the first confessional, the program's judges call the shots. There is only a chance of opening the vote to the audience if the panel's members deem it appropriate. It's a strategic measure to make sure none of the dangerous ones slip through. This year, the decision wasn't difficult. Having immediately expelled the contestants who protested about the use of high-pressure hoses after arriving on The Island, we already had four candidates to make up the final lineup of our Spanish-language edition. In this case, there would be no prior eliminations. I would have liked to see more disqualifications, but the Minister said no.

I must admit that, although I identified with him, I did nothing to help the Kid. I decided to apply the method I typically use so as not to implicate myself too much, thereby avoiding the sort of mistakes I had made in the past. On the other hand, I didn't cause him any problems. I refrained from recommending that fragments of his first public confessional should be leaked, although I knew they would boost our audience ratings. The contest's directors were the ones who decided to leak them after reading my transcriptions of his first statement. What I did do was participate actively in the programming board to make sure Nadir wouldn't be included in the second phase. I didn't like the cocky air he had about him. However much he had suffered as a homosexual prostitute, guys like him always end up becoming abusers.

It's not easy to justify that kind of decision, much less after what's happened. But the apocalyptic atmosphere that hangs over our times is so dense that it's impossible not to buckle under its weight. And anyway, everything is complicated in this business. In fact, it's hard for me to explain the circumstances that led to the creation of the contest. Even I don't know how to explain what happened. I only know that a big fence separates Europe's southern territories from the sea, and that *Immigration: The Contest* was born to bring in cheap labor while controlling the risk of waves of immigration. The candidates, all African immigrants, had to live together in a camp in full view of the whole audience.

I'm not entirely sure how many games of *Immigration* are being played at any given time in the newly re-established European Union. Nor in what language they take place. I know that, given the linguistic complexity of Europe, it didn't take long for editions of *Immigration* to be broadcast in the Union's various official languages. There were many versions, even in locations as isolated as my own. But I don't know about their frequency or the prize. Since I came to The Island, I have only received the news the producer sees fit to give me. I can only speak for myself. In our contest, only the winner is guaranteed access to the newly re-established Union, along with a work contract. Each language community programmed its edition according to its work offerings, as had always happened in Europe. Our Spanish-language edition, for example, had released twenty different seasons in a single year due to our labor needs; and with parallel editions broadcasting simultaneously, at that.

36

I know what I know because they gave me the opportunity to cover the contest for one of the Spanish-language editions. It took place on The Island, a speck of land halfway between Africa and Europe that had formed part of the country formerly known as Spain and had been adapted for use on the show. That's where the participants I worked with were housed. They all spoke Spanish, and they had reached the final phase after being selected based on their initial statements. I had to keep up to date with the confessionals that took place in that sector, and I was responsible for the challenges until the winner's name was made public.

When they offered me the job, I had my doubts. It wasn't my area. My girlfriend, who was already my ex-girlfriend back then, told me I was crazy to accept it. We had broken up a few weeks before, but we kept up a fluid relationship through email and social media. In fact, we broke up over social media when Ingrid published a message, tagging me, that said:

"i'm sorry but we can't go on. i don't love you anymore"

And those forty-three characters, released electronically into our circle of friends, were like a porcelain vase from a vanished culture that, after being placed in the most beautiful part of my house, had shattered into forty-three pieces before my eyes, and in that instant I knew I would never be able to put it back together or find another one like it. In order to get away from that message and the pain of the breakup, I escaped from the city that is no longer known as Hamburg, in the country that is no longer known as Germany, and I landed in this show. Here they just asked me to write: reports, scripts, interviews, challenge designs, outlines, as well as transcriptions of the most significant passages of the contestants' confessionals for broadcast. I thought a little silence and a lot of writing would help me put my life back together. It worked, but not for long. I started to forget about that age-old, broken porcelain vase. Nevertheless, two days ago I realized that the recovery process isn't over. Just after the tragedy, after exchanging a few messages on social media, I was overcome by an impulse I had controlled until that moment. I picked up my cell phone and called the city that is no longer known as Hamburg. I tried to get in touch with my ex-girlfriend to tell her what had happened.

For familial reasons, Ingrid is interested in lost causes and novels based on true stories. She's an expert on all the literature that's been written about the Holocaust, especially the works of W.G. Sebald. When we met, she was interested in me because she thought I could be useful to help her read the ample bibliography on the Spanish Civil War that fills that country's literature. This was the reason why we first struck up a conversation. Sadly, my knowledge of the subject hardly served her purposes.

Ingrid was indifferent to the subject of emigrants, on the other hand, despite her foreign origin. She didn't even take an interest in the anti-displacement protests organized by some of her friends, like her beloved Marliz. I should say that my ex-girlfriend is not an isolated case. More than a few citizens of the newly re-established European Union do the same thing: they sit at home in their ergonomic armchairs, comfortably settled in beside their vintage chimeneas, and enjoy reading those novels in which Nazism, Francoism, and other fascisms continue to appear as the only possible symbols of evil. If I were a moralist, and I'm not, I'd say they don't realize that this evil always develops thanks to the banality of those who look the other way.

It occurs to me that this is why no one has asked about the dark parts of this story. The well lit parts, on the other hand, the parts the producers use for the official version, are universally known in the newly re-established European Union; especially since the contest, using live transmissions of what happens in the sea surrounding southern Europe thanks to the technology developed by Silvio Pérez, made it possible to visually observe everything that's happening around The Island and its adjoining sets. The audience soon got used to the tower known as the "Eye of Europe." This was the robotic van-

38

tage point from which the Old Continent contemplated its waves of migration. Until recently, it was a lofty communications tower built on an abandoned islet in the middle of the sea, a structure that coordinates and distributes all video signal to the migration control centers, where the images are immediately sent off to be identified. That's how he took advantage of his investments in security for his business platform. He increased the audience ratings on his television channels, which monopolized the contest on channels that broadcast it live, and at the same time he obtained cheap labor for his industries. Not in vain, the winners immediately swelled the lines of his workers, all for a negligible wage. It was all done with a patina of consensus and democratic choice that made Pérez proud.

Things worked that way until two days ago, when the accident happened and they suspended all the editions of *Immigration*. It's worth mentioning that Pérez isn't entirely guilty. At least he's not the only one who's guilty. But it does seem evident that he has taken advantage of the circumstances to get rich off the suffering of others, televising this tear-inducing program that many of us workers refused to help broadcast, just as he took advantage of the contest for political gains.

This whole shameful farce, along with my deep sense of guilt after the accident and the failure of my first attempt to talk about the issue, has led me to make up my mind. I had to write the true story of *Immigration: The Contest*, or at least what I think was the true story of *Immigration: The Contest*, even if I wasn't so fond of all of its participants. 🖹

Name: Amina

Age: 28

Skin color: brown

Eye color: dark brown

Hair color: wears hijab

Profession: homemaker

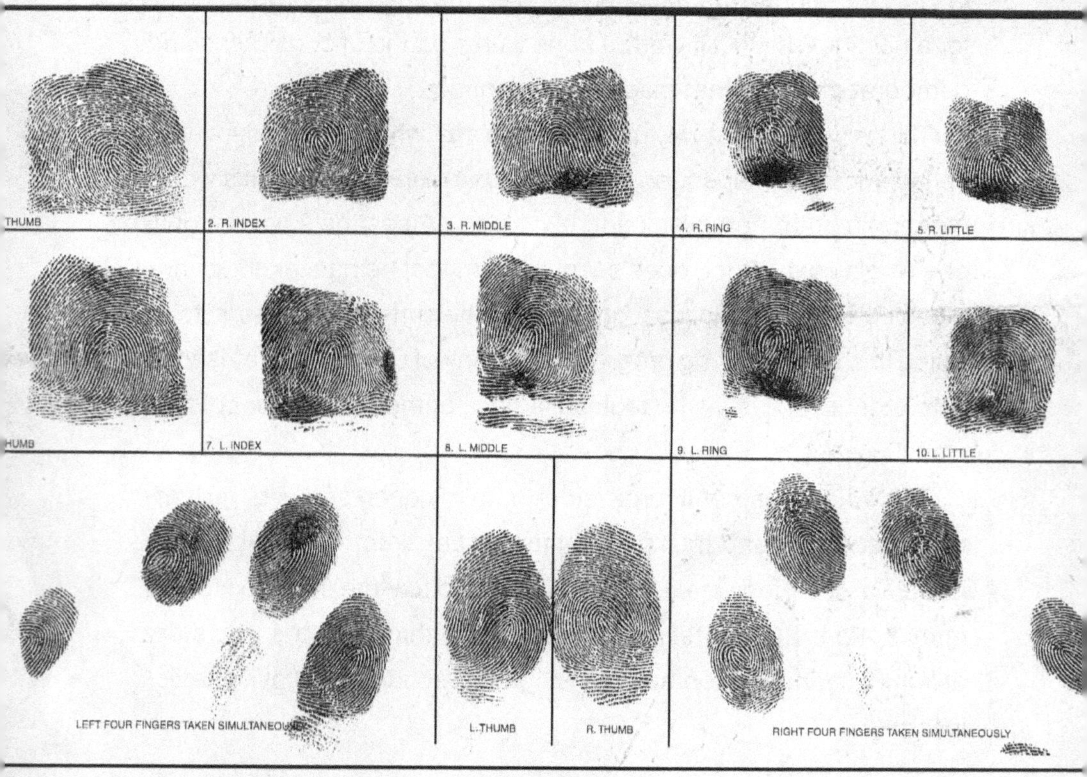

THUMB	2. R. INDEX	3. R. MIDDLE	4. R. RING	5. R. LITTLE
HUMB	7. L. INDEX	8. L. MIDDLE	9. L. RING	10. L. LITTLE

LEFT FOUR FINGERS TAKEN SIMULTANEOUSLY L. THUMB R. THUMB RIGHT FOUR FINGERS TAKEN SIMULTANEOUSLY

Sign--

The Mooress

THE WORST WAS A WHILE AGO, maybe six months: the challenge to get into the contest. Far away. But the hundred kilometers it takes to get to the city that is no longer Melilla are very hard. A hundred kilometers of straining your arms and legs to beat the challenge, always afraid of an accident.

It is different before. Travel in the transports. But one year these transports are freezers and all the participants are eliminated. They are frozen when they take them out. Poor little ones.

Another year the candidates travel on the roof of the transport. Better if the driver does not go too fast. But he does go fast and two contestants fly off on a curve. They crash into a light pole by the side of the highway. Just like that they are eliminated.

The challenges change every year, for the audience. This year too. The challenge is a surprise until the last minute. Then somebody from the organization tells us about it. I tell Aisha it is dangerous. The little girl competes by my side and travels with her grandmother. She sees when the old lady slips and we walk ten kilometers to pick the rest of her teeth out of her hair and clothes. I insist that children should not be allowed to compete. That you must be sixteen to participate. That it is difficult. That I spent a year on the challenges to be able to get here. But I say nothing about myself. Whatever happens will happen. I enter the contest after our misfortune and I reach the finale of the Spanish edition, this one, because Allah wills it.

I come to *Immigration* to find my sister. We are born twins at Kabylie. Our family lives close to the city that is no longer Tizi Ouzou, at the mountains. We move to other towns many times. I am not sure why. Until one day my mother gets tired and wakes up my sister and me in the night. She runs away with my sister. She tells me to go with them. But I stay because I love my father. I love his beard, even though it is not as long as it is now. I love his clothes, white as his pure heart. I love his smell, he smells like a man, like a good Muslim. Not like "the Kid," who says he's the same way, but who smells like western decadence.

When my mother escapes with my sister, my father is not as upright as he is now. He becomes very angry when he learns they run away. He almost hits me. I don't remember everything. I only remember the anger. But he tells me himself. I do remember that I love him. I also remember that after my mother and my sister run away, I want to forget them. Before, my mother complains a lot because she says that my father mistreats her. That he hits her and things like that. Maybe it is true because, like I say, I don't remember everything. But I do remember that my father changes. He becomes more serious. We do not move so much anymore through the towns at the mountains close to the city that is no longer Tizi Ouzou. Or we do it for other reasons, like when we go to the training camps. I can say that my father now has respect for his second and third wives. He says that ever since he follows the precepts of Islam he has learned to respect his women. That he does not do that with my mother. And he goes back to reading the sacred book: the Quran.

This is something that you westerners do not understand. That Muslim men are better with women if they follow Sharia. That when they do not, like my father at first, when my sister and I were born, they hit their wives, drink alcohol, take drugs, and sleep with whores, which is not the same as getting married many

42

times. This is why many women become fundamentalists and study Islamic law. Because that way they marry men who respect them because they follow the teachings of Sharia. You all think they hit them. And sometimes they do, but not always. This is something you never understand.

I grow up very happy with my father, his two wives, my four stepbrothers, and all the doubles of my village. I don't remember my sister at all. Until one day my father says that I must search for my sister and my mother. That he will not because he behaves badly with my mother when they live together. But it is different for me because she is my mother and because she is my sister. I do not want to go because I do not want to see my mother. But that same day I dream about my sister. The next morning my father says again that I must go and look for them. That my maternal aunt, who lived in the city that is no longer Algiers, has said that my sister is about to travel across the country. Then I think that everything, the sickness, the dream, my father's words, my sister and her journey, is the will of Allah. I decide to go.

I travel to the city where my aunt lives, to the medina. When I get there, my aunt says that my sister has left. That she has gone to do something with science or something like that. I am very surprised. I ask my aunt what my sister is like. I know she looks like me, but is not the same. She tells me everything, she even tells me what clothes she wears. I write down her words and I leave. The whole morning I walk around the medina and the souk, but I don't find her. I get tired of walking. The heat is stifling. I walk in front of the hammam. Since it is the day for women to bathe, I buy everything I need at the souk and go inside. I take my clothes off quickly. I massage my whole body. Then I sink into the little pool perfumed with rose water. I relax as I listen to the sound of the fountains and I smell the burning incense. When I am finished, I get out of the water and think I am looking at myself in a mirror.

I contemplate my skin, as pure as virgin silver. But it is not my skin because I am not in front of a mirror. I am in front of a foreign girl who smiles beside the washbasins.

We sit down together on the bench along the wall of the hammam. She gives me musk for my hair. I share henna for our fingernails. The young woman uses the henna to decorate her nails with the same symbol I have: II. It is not an Arabic symbol. It is a symbol my mother teaches us before she runs away. Few people know it. The young woman says her name is Ánima. She starts speaking Arabic, but she speaks badly and soon switches to French. She is born at this country, but she grows up in the country that is no longer France. She comes to the city that is not Algiers to finish I-don't-know-what. Something related with what she calls the great journey of humanity.

Ánima is beautiful. I want to brush my hand against her face. She talks about her life at the country that is not France. As a little girl she studies a lot. I tell her I also study a lot: I study the Quran. She says it is not the same. I understand that she is like you: a westerner. That is why she does not understand that studying the Quran can make your mind grow. But she does talk about science as if she talked about absolute truth. She explains that she works with genetics, I think. She says that genetics prove we are all the same. But she does not remember that scientists are the ones who invented races a century ago. Or that racists always talk about Darwin. That blasphemer who denies that man and woman are born at once from a drop of semen, as the Prophet affirms. She also forgets that now some biologists say that the Europeans and Asians have a good mixture of genes, but the blacks of Africa not so much. Racism again, but in another form. She does not know the words my father says the Imam says. That all the rich countries of the West start as fanatics: the Swiss Calvinists, the English and American Puritans, the Dutch Protestants. They all start by banning re-

44

ligions other than their own and killing those who oppose them. My father says the Imam says that later, with wealth, comes religious freedom, like it came to Islam at the start. That now we must be like those westerners: we must strictly follow Islamic law. That now wealth is returning to the Muslim countries. But I say nothing of this to my companion. She is a westerner, even if she looks like an Arab. She has bought a tourist t-shirt at the zoo with a phrase about the city that is no longer Algiers. When she puts it on she looks like one of those whores from FEMEN. She will not understand. I do not say anything. I just wave my hand when she leaves. Then I watch how a bit of paper falls out of her back pocket. She wears pants. Like I say, she is a westerner. I jump up from the bench and pick up the paper. I want to go after her and give it to her. Then at the hammam I run into another young lady I know from the mountains around the city that is not Tizi Ouzou. She is strict young woman. She tells me about a protest to support the religious martyrs at the country that is not Egypt. I join in. We go with twenty women in total. We block transport traffic and release balloons. We do no harm to anybody. But the police come. There are many police in the summer in the city that is not Algiers. Many tourists come from the newly re-established European Union and they have to watch out for their money, which goes to the government and not to the people. Soon more guards appear. They say we are bothering the tourists who drive around in rented transports. They arrest us all. They put us in cells. We are alone. We cannot speak to each other. I don't know what to do. I rummage through my clothes for the few possessions I have. I find the paper that fell to the floor from the woman in the hammam. I read it. In French it says something like:

This document certifies that Ánima Belmojtar, born Naï-ma Belmojtar, forms part of the scientific expedition "The

Great Journey of Humanity," as the biologist responsible for the genetic reconstruction of any human remains discovered.

I am speechless. The girl from the hammam is my sister Naïma. There can be no doubt. My name is Amina Belmojtar. She can be no other. I am surprised I did not recognize her. Now I understand the II symbol and why her skin is as pure as virgin silver. I also remember that my aunt says she was wearing pants. I am very happy and I would like to go and explain it to my father. But then I remember that I am in jail and I grow sad. I do not know if I can find my sister again.

One day they take us to the courtroom and read the sentence. They put on public executions in the summer because the tourists want to see things that do not exist in their country. The sentence is harsh. We are all condemned to die. I faint beside the defendants' bench. I wake up in my cell. Now I do not hear my companions. I think my fate is up to Allah. Then two guards walk in. They look at me with desire and I understand that I am the chosen one. Every summer, the police can choose a girl condemned to death to rape her. She is saved from death, but not from shame, which is worse. The guards drag me out and then I do hear my companion's moans. I scream as they carry me to the captain's office. He looks happy as soon as he sees me. He lifts my hijab to look at my hair. I am defenseless. He touches me. He grabs me through my clothes. He tries to raise my djellaba. The guards laugh. I am disgusted and ashamed. I also feel a dizziness I have not felt until now. Raped by a disgusting man in front of two others. My intimate parts exposed. I prefer to die over what it going to happen. Then I hear a loud noise. An explosion. The ground shakes and I know it is my father and his men, they do not abandon us. The captain leaves the office. The soldiers who take me there follow

46

him. I am cautious. I do not run toward the explosion. I take off my shawl, fold it, put it away, and then walk out. I hope Allah understands this sacrifice. I walk calmly in the opposite direction, away from the bomb. I cross paths with policemen who do not recognize me. I pass as a woman who works in the offices, hears the explosion and is afraid. They lead me to a military transport. I get in and we drive away from the station. From the transport I watch how some of my companions die from the gunshots of the police as they go running out of the hole the bomb left in the wall of the station. At the first stop, I get off the transport and blend in with the people. Many are worried about the bombs. There are dead women and children. Some say you cannot fight terror with terror. They talk like that French writer who betrayed us. They are outraged. But I think it is Allah's will and I lose myself in the streets around the medina.

I run away toward the mountains south of the city that is not Algiers. I know them well because we sometimes took trips there with my father. They are connected to the mountains of the city that is not Tizi Ouzou by the double highway. Also to the training camps. I know that when the summer passes there are not so many police because there are not so many tourists. Then you can take that route and some driver will give you a ride. You just have to wait to attempt the journey back. Months. But better that than being executed or raped. I walk away from the highway and through the mountains. I eat roots and wild fruits. I search for secret places to sleep. One day I find a camp. There wasn't one before. Black people there. They say they are there to do challenges for *Immigration: The Contest*. That day I find out it exists. They say they have already passed several stages and they can qualify. They are the ones who tell me about the different challenges with transports that go to the city that is not Melilla. They also talk about the fence challenge. Friends have told them it is better to go prepared be-

47

cause now the fence cuts when you jump it. They show me the gloves they have gotten so nothing bad happens to them. They mention the prize. They talk about an island in the sea where you live in luxury. They call it The Island of the Good Year. Very few make it there. For a moment I want to abandon my father and be one of them. I dream about living on The Island with my sister Naïma once I find her again.

I am in the camp for a few days. There I meet Cissé. He is kind, I tell him about the Quran. I try to convince him. But I run away because the contestants say many police are going to come, coming to make sure everything is in order. Maybe this time they are also looking for me. I must be cautious. When I am far enough away, I see a police transport going toward the camp. I hide myself in some brush and watch as they ask questions. It's not a normal control sweep for contestants, as I will discover later. They ask more questions and the young men respond by gesturing with their arms and hands. They point the opposite direction from the one I took. I give thanks to Allah. When they have no more questions, the agents beat the participants. Then they burn their shacks and push them all into the transport.

I stay hiding in the mountains. I go back to eating roots and wild fruits. That training serves me well later in the hard challenges of *Immigration*, like working in the field. I stay far away from the double highway until one day it storms and I must take shelter in a cave. There I find clues of the presence of men. Digging sticks and strange clamps. Then a lightning bolt strikes a tree and I know the summer has passed. I also know that Allah wants me to return. I am happy to think I can tell my father that I have found my sister at the hammam.

The next day, when it stops raining, I set out toward the double highway. It takes three days to reach it. But when I get there, I know that Allah is on my side. As soon as I set foot on the highway toward the city that is not Tizi Ouzou, I see a transport belonging to one of my father's allies. He comes from the training camps in the south. He is excited to see me and says that Allah is great. I say so too. I get in the transport and then he explains that they have not stopped taking action since the young women received their death sentence. He claims my father has been looking for me since the attack, when I disappeared. He tells me of offensives against the government and some actions against civilians. He says they have captured some westerners who are working in the mountains of the city that is not Tizi Ouzou when they find them. He says they form part of something to do with science. Then I remember the paper on the foreigner who I now know is my sister and also her words at the hammam. A cold sweat breaks out on my forehead, which is once again covered by my shawl. I take out the paper, which has been in my inner pocket the whole time. I ask if it is an expedition called "The Great Journey of Humanity." He says that he doesn't know, that these things are always happening at this country and they all have similar names. But they plan to kill them all in the same way they condemned the young women to death. My heart skips a beat. I keep thinking you can fight terror with more terror. But I also ask him to speed up.

In a few hours we will be at my father's house. I get out of the transport with the paper at my hand. I find my father. He appears in the door of one of the village's houses with a strange look on his face. Then he is very happy to see me. I tell him that I think my sister is among the foreigners. He answers that this is impossible. That there is only one woman and her name is not Naïma. But I show him the paper so he can read it. Then his face changes and he fears the worst. He kneels, moans, cries. He tears up the paper in anger. He beats his chest and shouts: Dishonor, dishonor. I don't understand what is happening to him. But then I hear other cries, different from my father's. They come from a half-open door in the house he came out of. I walk toward them and when I open the door I see her: the foreigner from the hammam who is my sister. Naked. Her hair is shaved and she is lying on a bed. She hides her breasts with her arms. Again I contemplate that skin as pure as virgin silver and the II symbol marked with henna on her fingernails. She is also shaved below and she has bite marks on her body. Then I find out why she cries. She has been raped. Raped by her own father, who is my father, in the presence of two combatants, after watching the torture and death of her companions. I tell her we are sisters. She does not respond. She is stunned. I remember the fear and disgust I felt in the office of the captain of the guard while he took off my shawl. For a few seconds I think like that French writer, that you can't fight terror with more terror. Then I think it is Allah's will and I go to console my father. He has changed his orders. My sister was going to die as an infidel, in this way she would pay for the executed women. But if I am alive, she must also live.

For a week we go back to being the family we were. The problems come back. My father does not speak. He has shaved his beard and cut his hair in penance. My sister does not speak either. I want to communicate with her like at the hammam, but she runs away from me. I tell her about the island in the middle of the sea that the contestants I found in the mountains told me about. I think it is the only place where we can live now. But she does not answer. The only time she speaks, she asks if what has happened to her is what I want for women who do not think like me. I want to answer with my memory of the cells in the city that is not Algiers, but I keep quiet. A week later she is gone. I ask my father and he says she cannot live with us any longer, that it is bad for the group, that we are going to extend our operations into other countries and Naïma gets in our way. He has banished her from the village and separated us again. I think he has taken her to the city that is not Algiers. There is no proof. My father says she is sick like me, he says one sick person in the family is enough. This time I am the one who gets angry. Very angry. With my father. I do not answer. The next day I run away. I go back to the city that is not Algiers. I go to my aunt's house. I find out that my sister has not been here. I spend weeks looking for her in other cities. I do not find her. I have no idea where she has gone. I suppose she returns to Europe. Then I decide to prepare for the contest. I want to go to Europe too. I think about The Island of the Good Year and I head to one of the training camps I know.

One day I think I am ready. I get the necessary information and I learn how to avoid the police checkpoints. I speak good French as well as Arabic. I decide that I learn Spanish talking to the participants in the show. I sign up and I present myself at the qualifying challenge. There I find Aisha, the little girl who travels with her grandmother who later loses her teeth. Then we find out that we must travel a hundred kilometers. That is our qualifying challenge: a hundred kilometer journey to the contestant admission center at the city that is not Melilla but at the back of the transport. A hundred kilometers of straining your arms and legs, with your nails broken from grabbing so hard at the bars. Also being very careful not to touch the wheel axles with your feet. Not like Aisha's grandmother, who loses her balance, hits the axle and ends her journey with no teeth and eliminated. That is one of the strong emotions the audience wants. I have to hold on to the little girl for the whole journey. I also dry her tears while I wipe the drops of her grandmother's blood off my clothes. Luckily, I am ready for similar challenges thanks to the information from the contestants that I meet at the mountain. Also thanks to my training at the camps. Not Aisha. When we can barely see the lights of the city that is not Melilla she tries to jump off. She slips out of exhaustion. I grab her by her hair, so the wheels do not destroy her. But she takes a strong

51

blow on the back and her legs are caught in the axles and broken in several places. The transport stops. They say that Aisha is not eliminated because children cannot compete. But they did not mind charging her the sign-up fee. The girl writhes in pain. A doctor says she will never walk again. She will be in a wheelchair forever. The show's cameras capture the image, which is hellish. But it was written. The misfortune is the will of Allah.

I qualify. At the contestant center of the city that is no longer Melilla, I find Cissé. We are happy to find each other after so many challenges. He introduces me to Mamadou, but he calls him another name. Through him, Mamadou and I make friends. That is why I try to convince Mamadou to convert to Islam when he is afraid during his journey to The Island. Then Cissé explains that the day the police come to the camp they take them into the desert because the show's organization has decided they need an extra challenge to qualify. Cissé tells me that challenge is another year's journey.

We are lucky because they take us to The Island of the Good Year. A tear falls down my cheek when I see it from the sea. I am so happy that I don't care when they tell us the trip itself is a special challenge. I don't care when they spray us with hoses in the mornings. I don't care about the daily mini-challenges. A big surprise awaits me on the island, the one I wish for the most. But also a disappointment. It happens after I pass the qualifying challenge, which I don't know how I pass because in the first weeks it is still very hard for me to speak Spanish. So much that the people laugh at my Spanish because they imagine that learning many languages is easy. But they only know one. Later it is better. I do well in the police challenge. The audience likes my performance. The politician who comes to visit us even congratulates me and says she knows my sister. That gives me a lot of votes. My team wins the challenge where we have to work in the fields with the help of my experience and Mamadou's muscles. The Kid can do nothing. He is not ready to work in such heat. I also meet the Kid in the contestant center in the city that is not Melilla. But I know he is trash from the first time I meet him. At first I do nothing because, after seeing what happens with the hose showers, I don't want them to disqualify me. But then I bother the Kid as much as I can. I put needles in his bed at night and I touch the things in his locker. His words about Africans, which we can all hear at a special episode, make me angry. I don't know how he is able to say he is a good Muslim. He makes me sick. People like the Kid do not deserve to live at Africa. They should all be killed for being depraved and corrupt. But I am not to blame for his sickness, as even the audience says. At least, I am not to blame in the way they say. But I will not say I don't really know why. But now I am here, at the finale at The Island of the Good Year, which I hope to win. ⌗

This was the confessional of Amina, known among the audience as The Mooress. In her first statement we could hardly understand a thing; just the words "rape" and "police," and it wasn't clear who had been the victim, her or her sister. Back then, her Spanish was even more limited. Even her final speech wasn't completely clear, and this conditioned both the events themselves and the audience.

I've already said that Amina really passed the first challenge because, after disqualifying the four participants who had protested against the hoses, we had ended up with just the right number of finalists. I thought we had a good opportunity to reduce the number of contestants to three, ending up with our tightest, most competitive season to date. I put forth a proposal that suggested eliminating whomever had performed worst in the first confessional, which was none other than Amina. But the Minister of Integration turned it down. I don't know why she decided to save her. I don't think the Minister was overly moved by her words, although she was certainly moved when Amina pulled off that brilliant performance during the police checkpoint challenge. The images of the young woman carrying herself with brusque confidence in front of the other contestants almost reduced her to tears. But that happened much later.

I, on the other hand, hated Amina. I'm sure she hated me too. Nonetheless, just like with the Kid, I tried to apply my special method in her confessionals so the hate would not affect me, and also so as to draw the greatest possible media impact from her words.

I had decided to use this strategy after the second season. At the time, I was getting on well with one of the participants, a Saharan girl called Salma. Back then I always watched the contestants' faces while I spoke to them during the first public confessional. We would record fragments of their declarations after I read them a series of subjects to open up about as they shared their opinion of Europe, so they would be more comfortable while they made their statement. While I read, I tried to look them square in the face in the hopes that my hospitality would flow into them through their retinas. That was how I interacted with Salma. As soon as I saw her eyes and contemplated those eyelids and those eyelashes, I knew I liked her. A few days later, I decided to talk to her on a more intimate level. She had realized I was fascinated by her. More often than not, a flash of smiling eyes accompanied her sweet voice. She seemed to be inviting me to come closer, and that meant a lot to me. My breakup with my ex-girlfriend had been hard on me, and flirting with Salma comforted me like a blanket by the fire after a long journey through the snow. Even if it was impossible to put my antique porcelain vase back together, perhaps I could create something just as delicate with Salma. Nonetheless, I didn't want to get my hopes up. Her magnetism toward me was no different from her magnetism toward the rest of the team, all of which was entranced by her, just like the audience, which adored her. She was helped along by the color of her skin, a brown that reminded one a great deal of the skins you can still see in the country that is no longer known as Spain; also by her accent, a perfect, tipsy Spanish; and her nationality, as more than a few citizens of the country no longer known as Spain love Saharans just as they hate their northern neighbors from the Maghreb.

In short, one got the impression that Salma had exactly what everyone wants in a foreigner: the right dose of exoticism without threatening one's own culture. That's why she was the favorite of that season, which she won with ease. She won thanks to her "sex appeal." It wasn't clear to what extent I was involved.

56

That same season, I had put a contestant from Morocco through some rough treatment. He said he had worked in recently re-established Europe and slept with his boss's wife, which he bragged about publicly. If we are to take his words literally, they expelled him for fucking the boss lady in the ass. His name was Mimoun.

I couldn't stand the guy's authoritarian behavior, so I gave him all the hardest questions. I did so to fight back against the machismo of his actions, starting with the look with which he undressed me when we met in the confessional room and ending with the story about his boss.

The day of his first confessional, I came up with a list of issues that would paint a picture of Mimoun for the viewers. I took advantage of my creative freedom to include my own suggestions on the subjects proposed by the program's directors. I imagined they would affect the audience's considerations. And so it was. It became clear that Mimoun's attitudes were terribly, archaically machista, that he thought Muslims were superior and European society ought to change instead of him. By the next week, he was already out of the contest. The judges didn't even think it was necessary to take a vote and they eliminated him. Given his attitude since he arrived on The Island, it wasn't exactly a hard choice.

On the other hand, I always proposed questions to Salma that I knew would boost the audience's opinion of her. I gave her more and more suggestions as the program progressed. This drew us closer together. As much as I could, I helped Salma in all the challenges she had to overcome. Especially in the final statement, when I tried to correct her accent and I taught her phrases that would make her more appealing to the audience. I also recommended that the production team use shots that showed her good side. I wanted her to win.

From our times together, I still remember her touch and the feeling of her skin, which was a flow of electric current passing through my body. I used to come back from those encounters completely wet.

I thought we had established a bond that would continue when the contest was over. But, once she received the prize, her attitude changed abruptly. I wanted to hug her to celebrate her victory at the door of The Island minutes before the boat came to take her to Europe, but she moved away from me. It was the first time we saw each other after the finale. I understood that she had used me. My relationship with Salma, which I imagined could transform into a bright new work of art under my care, was not going to take shape after that ship arrived. I don't know why, but I thought about Arale.

My teenage years weren't easy. I was hung up for a long time because of my body. Back then I felt like a robot, incapable of interacting with other people—especially with girls, who were the only people who interested me. Since I was insecure and conflictive at home, besides all that, my parents took me to a psychologist.

I guess my mother, informed by the psychologist, found out how I felt, because she gave me two recommendations. The first was a book: *I, Robot*, a novel by Isaac Asimov whose title gave me great expectations. I thought that, through reading, I would discover the emotivity of these robots whom I considered my brothers and sisters. Nonetheless, it turned out to be a huge letdown. More than a science fiction book, it was like a puzzle that had to be solved logically according to the rules provided at the beginning of the text. Just what I needed least at that moment of emotional fragility. Luckily, I was able to find refuge in my mother's other piece of advice: the series *Dr. Slump*, whose Catalan-language version I found on YouTube. Arale Norimaki became the perfect character for me. She had undefined sexuality, a robust body, and uncommon strength. Her relationship with her father, who was her inventor, seemed as strange as my own. But, above all, she was naïve.

Through Arale, I regained the hope in robotics I had lost after reading Asimov. I bought several t-shirts printed with her image, and I even

58

started a collection of products and merchandise bearing her name. Thanks to that, I made new friends. They were attracted by my fondness for Arale. And they associated my problematic shyness with an attempt to imitate the cartoon character, so I ended up seeming as nice to them as she did.

I remember how my ex-girlfriend thought all the Norimaki products I treasured were so funny, but I didn't remember Arale when my relationship with Ingrid and my antique porcelain vase broke apart with that public message of forty-three characters. I did remember her, on the other hand, when Salma left. The rejection I felt on the dock of The Island led me to recall the complexes I had suffered in adolescence due to my body. But this time, I felt wounded by my own lack of professionalism. I thought I had been undertaking my interviews without a biased gaze when, in reality, I was conditioning the contest.

I'm no standard-bearer for anti-racism, but when I was a teenager, despite my complexes, I suffered something similar to what the young people who are admitted to Europe through *Immigration* suffer, once again because of my appearance.

My father comes from the south of the country that is no longer known as Spain, although my mother is Catalan, and from him I inherited those morisco traits that once embarrassed me as much as the rest of my body. I have a hooked nose, jet black hair, black eyes, and dark skin. The police mistrusted my physical appearance and often stopped me on the street. First they asked for my documents, and then they waited to hear my accent to make sure I was European. In the country no longer known as Spain, the issue was settled when they heard me speak and confirmed my nationality. After all, more than a few members of the police force have the same traits as me and an identical skin tone. The problem centered on the confluence between my sexuality and their machismo. More than one cop tried to cross the line, exploiting the slightest glimmer of a doubt about my origin.

Everything was different when, years later, I moved to the country that is no longer known as Germany. There they had great respect for my borderline sexuality, but not so much for my skin, which they saw as an insuperable barrier on which each of my pores represented a virus ready and waiting to infect their society. For that reason, besides occasional police stops, I also had to show the inside of my bag at supermarket checkouts, confirm my financial history in the bank, and take every last item out of my suitcase every time I took a plane. In fact, in the country that is no longer known as Germany, they placed much more importance on a person's origin, which saved me since, when they identified me, I always appeared in the law enforcement computers as a person of Iberian origin (either Catalan or Spanish, which wasn't clear back then). This ended up putting the guards at ease. The other daily scenes were the ones that kept me from living a calm, everyday life. I understand what happened to the Turks, who were expelled en masse, even though some intellectuals of Ottoman origin had defended the German cause to other migrants in the past. Of course, if I were the memorialist I'm not, I would say their task was one of forgetting, because more than a few Jews fought on the German side during the First World War, renouncing their religion and identity traits and publicly backing the society that had taken them in. But that didn't exempt them from the agonies of Nazism.

I've always taken all of this into account, and it was important for me to prepare confessionals that didn't imply prejudices about the contestants' traits. I thought I was doing it right. Through Salma and Mimoun, I realized this was not so.

Then I promised not to let myself be deceived by appearances. Of course, I had the option of directing the confessionals from the control room. Nonetheless, I preferred a higher level of contact. I know my presence distorted these encounters, but listening to the other is the only possible way of understanding him, and one tends to believe that that's important in this line of work. So I came up with a method for the

60

interviewees that involved never looking the speaker in the eye, listening to their voice without seeing their face. I went into the confessional room before the contestants were given access, I always placed the chair with its back facing the spot where the camera pointed, and I waited for the next contestant to come in. When the participants arrived in the room, I was already there, and they greeted me. I returned the greeting. Then, always with my back to them, I outlined my suggestions in a neutral and un-emphatic tone while the camera captured the images I would later select.

There can be no doubt that audio is less manipulable than visuals. If you see the image after hearing the word, or if you omit the image in order to focus on the word, it's much more difficult to fall into a ruse like Salma's. Nonetheless, you've already read the lies hidden behind the Kid's first confessional. And Amina seems to live in a perpetual state of suspicion. She has always given the impression of hiding something, a secret that the members of the program team never came to know. This was accentuated when we learned of a series of unexpected facts in the confessional from the next woman character: the girl who came from one of the French editions, whom we had swapped for Cissé. A person with a high level of intellectual development. Although Ánima didn't always behave like an intellectual, as we later learned. But you'll know all about that after reading the confessional I'll share with you tonight. 田

Name: Ánima

Age: 28

Skin color: brown

Eye color: dark brown

Hair color: black

Profession: scientist

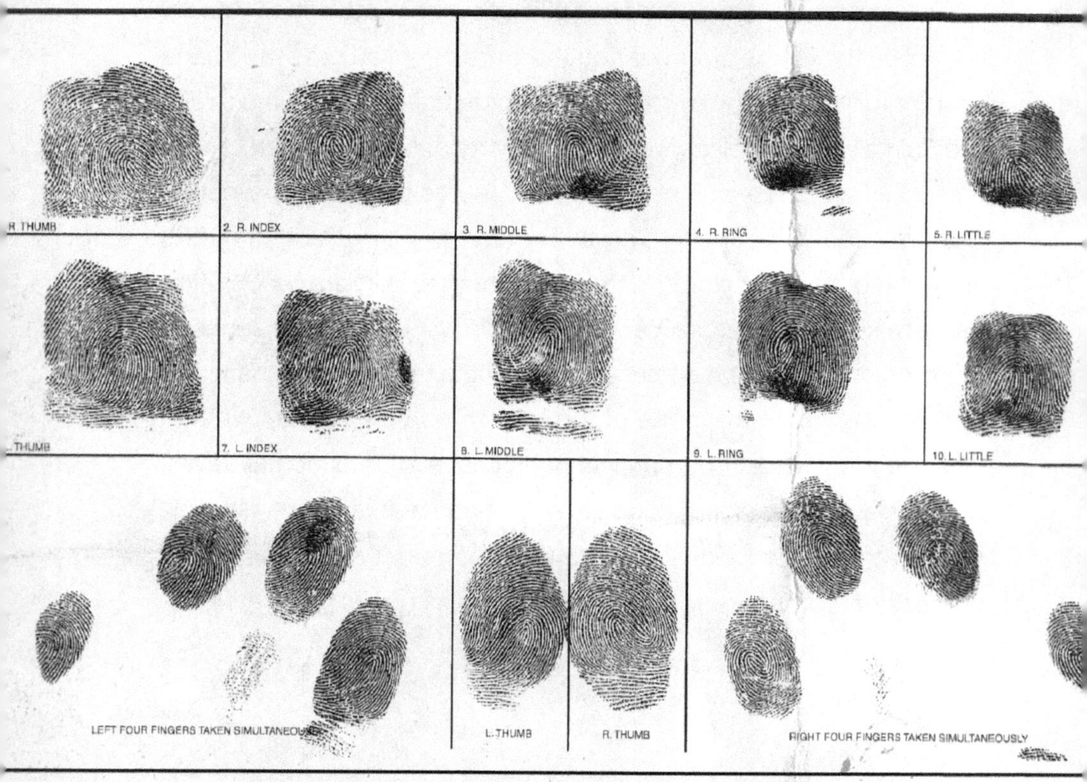

R. THUMB	2. R. INDEX	3. R. MIDDLE	4. R. RING	5. R. LITTLE
THUMB	7. L. INDEX	8. L. MIDDLE	9. L. RING	10. L. LITTLE

LEFT FOUR FINGERS TAKEN SIMULTANEOUSLY	L. THUMB	R. THUMB	RIGHT FOUR FINGERS TAKEN SIMULTANEOUSLY

Sign_____

The wise woman

I ARRIVE ON THE ISLAND BY SURPRISE. I come from another elimination round where I have a chance at winning. But I fear that my past in the country formerly known as France might turn things against me and I decide to change places with a contestant from the Spanish-language edition. À chacun son destin.

I'm a European. I lived almost all of my childhood and all of my adolescence here. I studied at university here. And I was a nationalized European when the recently re-established Union decreed the expulsion of foreigners. The fact is, by then, I was already working with a team of researchers on a project financed by European funds. This was one of the reasons they respected my nationality and my mother's, in spite of our origin. But, in a fit of rage, my father tore up the last piece of paper that certified my identity as a European. They took the rest, my passport and my other documents, and they burned them when they kidnapped us. So the authorities of the newly re-established European Union don't believe I am who I say I am. They say I could be faking it, even though I'm the last survivor of a kidnapping. They claim acting schools have cropped up across the area, schools where migrants go and rehearse in hopes of making themselves pass as others, and they don't grant me asylum. That's when I decide to enter this contest. It's the only way to get my life back in the country formerly known as France.

After requesting my transfer, I find my sister: Amina. To my surprise, our reunion takes place on this imaginary island she mentioned as the only place we could ever coexist. She is dumbstruck when she sees me. But I immediately understand that her idyllic perspective was false. What she said was going to become a bucolic existence transforms into a competition between us. This is the fact that corroborates my doubts about the claims I heard coming out of her mouth in the mountains around the city formerly known as Tizi Ouzou, a place of sad memories for me. Not only because of what happened there what must have been a year ago. Also because of my childhood. Because of the merciless beatings my father gave my mother. Because of the strange way he touched my sister and me. And because of the continuous movement of our whole family through the different villages where my father sold his wares. It was tobacco, as I remember; my mother claimed it was more dangerous stuff. But one day my mother gets tired of it and I leave with her. *Au revoir papa.* My sister stays. She says she's not leaving when we try to pull her out of bed. When her mama tells her to come with us, she says she loves her papa. I think she's crazy. And I imagine the beating she's going to receive from my father when he finds out about our escape.

The journey from there is slow. First we arrive at the house of my aunt, my mother's sister, in the city formerly known as Algiers. She is outraged when she sees the marks left on my mother's face by my father's last beating. She says my mother has to leave him. And she invites us to stay and live with her. My mother agrees. They send me to school in Algiers for a year. The fact is, I had never set foot in a school before then. The teacher helps me a lot. He says I'm a brilliant student and he talks to my mother. After two years, he convinces her to move us to the country formerly known as France. My teacher says I'll have more opportunities to go to university there. So we move to the area formerly known as the Banlieue, now the Peripheric Conurbation of the Parisian Region. There we find out that my father has given up smuggling and become a member of Islamic terrorist groups. His photograph appears in all the newspapers of the country formerly known as France. So we forget about him, his beatings and his abuse, and we settle in the suburbs of the city formerly known as Paris. There are many immigrants, so the relationship with the natives isn't good. They accuse us of stealing their wealth even though my mother wakes up early every day to go to work. She feels lost here, but I don't. I enroll in the public Lyceum. It's a huge building attended by students from various communities within a wide area. My studies go well. But since I'm an immigrant, I always have more to prove than the other kids at school. Especially in front of two of my classmates, two twins who treat me with scorn, daughters of the head of a famous anti-immigrant party. They're two years older than me. They've had to repeat various courses. They say this is because of the frequent trips they take with their father. But I think they're just bad students. One day, one of them, the one who's in my class, tells me her father says immigrants should live in concentration camps so as not to spoil the cityscape. *Mon Dieu!* What she doesn't say is that, thanks to the lower-class white votes from my neighborhood, they get to live in an exclusive area inaccessible to many of their own voters. But, instead of speaking, I keep my mouth shut and start crying. That day I get the highest grade in the class in natural sciences. To my great surprise, many years later I find myself face to face with her twin sister on The Island. She has come to watch a special episode of the contest. She's the new Minister of Integration of the newly re-established European Union, and I crack a smile when I find out.

The fact is, my childhood confrontations with the two sisters bring out the best in me. I'm the number one student at my school. At the age of twelve, I'm so well integrated that I start leaving all the symbols of Islam at home. I change my name. I decide to call myself Ánima instead of Naïma. I think it expresses my personality

65

better. I set Arabic aside and always speak French. I embrace the republican ideology they instill in the classroom. I know "La Marseillaise" by memory. I go to school dressed like any other French girl, and my teachers are very happy. I understand that when the system gives you something, you usually end up wanting it. But they find a strange genetic trait in me. I'm a carrier of a hereditary abnormality that suggests my future descendants will always be products of twin embryos, either fraternal or identical. My mother says I got it from my father. It's not clear if it's caused by contact with one of the drug addicts he had dealings with in my childhood, or if my father transmitted it to me himself, since he is also a carrier. Either way, the news is devastating for my mother. I'm not entirely sure why. It doesn't seem so serious to me. So I get over it and decide to study biology. Genetics, to be exact, in order to try to research the reasons behind and possible treatments for this trait. Thanks to the grant program of the country formerly known as France, I am able to make my dream a reality. Soon, I join a research lab. There I learn about the nature of the project, "The Great Journey of Humanity," for the first time. It's related to a theory that's very much in vogue at the time, the so-called "Out of Africa" theory. Given my condition as an immigrant, I am fascinated by the hypothesis, which is gaining traction in comparison to others at the time. Nonetheless, I am still interested in researching the genetics of the parents of twins. In the end, I am finally convinced by a story I hear from a Brazilian labmate.

It's the story of a Nazi war criminal, a former collaborator of Josef Mengele. My labmate asks if I'm an identical twin. I suppose he asks due to my genetic abnormality and the line of work that interests me. I tell him no, I have a fraternal twin sister in the country formerly known as Algeria. We look alike but we're not identical. Then he says it's better that way. But he's still unsure whether or not Mengele or his collaborator, Dr. Zwilling, would

66

have left us alone if they'd met us. And he tells me about this criminal, a doctor based at Auschwitz who helped Mengele experiment on Jewish identical and fraternal twins—and who, as such, would have been happy to practice on twins of migrant origin like my sister and me. Mengele hated racial mixing and sent the young women who got pregnant with the German guards' babies to the gas chambers. It's possible that Dr. Zwilling felt the same way. But he was interested in twins for the sake of increasing the reproductive rates of the Aryans. My labmate explains that the Nazis thought they were Aryans, a supposed master race established by natural selection, and that they shouldn't mix with others. A theory that has certain parallels to the anthropological hypothesis of multiple origins, according to which *Homo sapiens* emerges at the same time in different parts of the planet, giving rise to the existence of distinct races. At the time, that was the theory that competed with ours.

Zwilling followed in Mengele's footsteps and fled to South America with the help of the Nazi support networks woven after the Second World War. And also thanks to a young Jewish woman from the Red Cross whom he seduced in order to avoid the suspicions of the Allied soldiers in Genoa. From there, he took a ship to Argentina. He carried Mengele's briefcase, which he had recovered, risking his life by returning to Auschwitz to search for it in spite of the Russian occupation. It is thought that his purpose was to return it to its owner, and that was why he travelled with it to South America.

Zwilling was hiding from the Nazi-hunters, moving between Uruguay, Paraguay, and Argentina. Just when they were about to trap him in Paraguay, he decided to flee to Brazil. By chance, he came to the little town of Villa Godói. It just so happens that there's a strange story behind that place. They say it's the town with the highest number of twins in Brazil. And this is because in that town, in hiding, Mengele continued with his experiments. But it has been proven that the Nazi doctor was never there, so my labmate thinks the true culprit was Zwilling with Mengele's briefcase.

My labmate explains that he travelled to Villa Godói. He formed part of the team of geneticists sent to refute the hypothesis that linked the place to Mengele. He says they proved it had nothing to do with that Nazi war criminal, nor with Zwilling. The twins were the result of the endogamy that prevailed in the region, which made certain genes common when they would normally be rare. But he also explains that the place is quite mysterious. One in five births produces twins, but that's not all. Everything in that place is duplicated. When my labmate arrived in the village, his team was received by two parallel boys on two parallel bicycles. One image was the exact copy of the other. He thought he was dreaming when he confirmed that the trees by the doors of the houses, like the residences themselves, were made up of identical pairs, which are clearly abnormal in nature; and that the flowers grew in doubles, sprouting one beside the other, always the same size. The calves were also born twins. The stray cats roamed in pairs with the same patches on their flanks. And the town was famous for producing a cereal variant with two grains, always identical. My labmate confirms that this has nothing to do with Nazi experiments. None-theless, he also says the place holds something mysterious, some-thing frightening. It's no surprise that a guy who's fascinated by Zwilling's experiments on twins should be attracted to Villa Godói. It was the doppelgänger paradise.

That's where Zwilling's trail goes cold until he reappears in the outskirts of São Paulo, where he had fled after breaking away from the other former members of the Nazi party. According to my labmate, the final witnesses say he was in financial ruin. He was living in a favela. He was reported by a neighbor after under-taking an operation on a teenage girl who later died. Some say it

68

was an abortion. Others say he was actually helping her give birth to twins. It's not clear. He was arrested and served a sentence of two years. In prison, he ended up writing a medical treatise in which he sought to prove his theories about the purity of the Aryan race. Zwilling would die years later from a heart attack with the briefcase by his side. The Brazilian police confiscated it immediately.

A new edition of Zwilling's book had a certain resonance in Brazilian universities just when my labmate was finishing up his doctoral studies. He remembers that this is what convinced him to keep investigating the hypothesis of the African origin of *Homo sapiens*, which is currently the theory most strongly supported by empirical evidence. The fact is, the day I hear the story, it occurs to me that the genetics of the parents of twins seems to have been thoroughly studied already, and I understand that perhaps there is no future for me in that field. Then I remember my classmate: the girl whose father was the head of the most famous anti-immigrant party in the country then known as France. And I want to believe that the hypothesis of the African origin is correct. That we are all descended from the same father and the same mother. That we all emerged from the same place and were then scattered by fate. And I want to believe it because the recent expulsions of immigrants have stirred up the spirits of Europe's population. I have nightmares that night. I dream about my sister. Dr. Zwilling is coming after us, he wants to kill us to carry on with his experiments. I wake up afraid. I decide I'm going to work on this theory, to prove that it's true. And I apply for a position as a geneticist on the project. Before long they confirm my spot as the researcher in charge of the genetic reconstruction of the archaeological remains of human beings used in the project titled "The Great Journey of Humanity." I have to draw out haplotype trees and phylogeographic analyses of the samples they give me. These diagrams are no less than the fixed picture of our genes and the sequence of how they have moved across the planet.

One day they get us together to tell us we're going to make a move to the country formerly known as Algeria. We have to confirm the recent theories sustaining that there was more than one journey, up to a total of four, coinciding with climate changes associated with variations in Earth's orbit, which indicate migrations across the pre-coastal area of the Maghreb. My contribution consists of collecting samples of human remains for later analysis in the lab.

When we arrive at the city formerly known as Algiers, I head to my aunt's house. She's the only person in our place of origin with whom we've kept in touch. My aunt is happy to see me and we talk for a long time. I give her a quick explanation of the scientific project in which I'm participating. But I don't ask her about my sister or about my father. I feel a certain uneasiness. To ward it off, I decide to go to the hammam after leaving my aunt's house. I go as just another tourist, since going to the Turkish bath is no longer a habit of mine. On the way, in the souk, I buy a souvenir t-shirt of the city that is not Algiers. At the hammam, I meet a young woman. She never reveals her name. Now I know she was my sister. But at the time, it doesn't even cross my mind. I haven't seen her in many years. And, the fact is, she carries herself with caution. It seems like she's afraid of sharing information. Nevertheless, she's willing to share other things with me, which strikes me as odd. Not only do we share the musk I bought on the square and the henna she brought, we also share the symbol with which we decorate our fingernails: II. It's a symbol I learned from my mother, and my sister hasn't forgotten it.

I decide to dust off my Arabic with her. But a moment later we've sunken into a dialectical battle and I return to French. She tries to match my academic efforts with her Quranic studies. *Mon*

70

Dieu! She tries to counter the universal, altruistic discourse of science with the localist, biased arguments of religion. She doesn't even miss a beat when I explain that contemporary genetics has nothing to do with pseudoscientific racist discourses. At that moment, I think of Mengele and Dr. Zwilling. I get angry and I tell her my project proves that all of humanity comes from Africa. That our mitochondrial Eve and chromosomal Adam were born there. That the theory is strongly corroborated. And that we are investigating the various movements of our ancestors from the African continent. I don't perceive even the slightest sign of emotion in her, even when I tell her that these journeys put the very survival of our species at risk, that we are here today thanks to them. That's why I don't believe even a word of what she says after. I'm not interested in what she has to say about the English Puritans and other nonsense. Minutes later I'm going to run into her again, cutting off my vehicle's path in a violent protest. She and her companions throw blunt objects at the drivers of individual transports until the police arrive and arrest her. I see how they carry her away in handcuffs along with many other men and women.

The fact is, the moment I watch how they clear away the rioters is when I realize I don't have my ID document on me. At first I think I've left it in the hotel. Or that I absent-mindedly dropped it. But now, after what's going to happen in the mountains, I grow ever more certain that my sister stole it from me. That's why they found out what we were doing and came after us. The excuses she will give me later mean nothing to me. That's why I'm so cold to her when I come to the Spanish-language edition of the contest.

That afternoon, after confirming the loss of my safe-conduct, I meet up in the hotel lobby with the other members of the expedition to swap opinions. We work as a team. They explain the details of our research to me. Until now, the possibility that North Africa had something to do with "The Great Journey of Humanity"

71

has been disregarded. But recently discovered human remains in the country formerly known as Algeria, between 190,000 and 40,000 years old, have changed this perspective. Some scientists have put forth the hypothesis that North Africa was the first area where *Homo sapiens* set foot after leaving the heart of the African continent and crossing the Arabian Peninsula. Others say one of the possible exit journeys took place across Sinai. Paleoclimatic data and a few genetic analyses seem to suggest they're right. I'm here to prove it. I'm the one who must identify the series of genetic elements that allow us to establish our origin.

When the meeting ends, I approach my labmate, Euclides, the Brazilian biologist who told me the story of Dr. Zwilling. I explain to him that I've lost my ID document. He tells me not to worry and invites me to take a ride in a private transport through the city formerly known as Algiers. We have dinner in a restaurant by the sea. We eat sole in a *sauce meunière délicieux*. Over dinner, he tells me about his research trip to the Horn of Africa. On that journey, they verified the theory that one of the hominid groups that left the African continent behind, from whom we are descended, departed from that area. Euclides speaks of the small group of individuals who set forth on the journey. According to him, genetic tests analyzing the entire global population show that a large measure of the inhabitants of other continents come from a quite specific branch. At least this is what the genetics and the haplotype trees reveal. That means, apparently, that a large number of us non-Sub-Saharans are descendants of a single tribe. It was a tribe that abandoned its African habitat owing to a drought or food shortage; a group of hominids who crossed the Red Sea over the Horn of Africa and ventured into the country formerly known as Yemen, then crossed the Arabian Peninsula in search of supplies and resources; a tribe capable of putting together an incredibly risky plan in order to improve its future and that of its children. It's something very human,

72

something very specific to *Homo sapiens*, my labmate says. And I am moved by the thought of this small group of migrants, this band of men, women, and children who changed the course of history and of our survival as a species. And, in my mind, I reconstruct this journey that allowed the human race to expand throughout the planet. And I think of my mother fleeing the village where we lived with my father. And of the boat that carried us to the country formerly known as France. And a tear runs down my cheek.

The next morning, we set out for the mountains. After hearing what I heard from my sister's lips in the hammam, I decide to put on a hijab. That way I won't call attention to myself and I'll avoid problems with the natives.

In the mountains, we find out about the terrible attack that takes place in the city formerly known as Algiers. Not from the Internet, because we don't have coverage, but thanks to the satellite dishes of the small town residents who give us shelter. I am horrified by the terrible images that accompany the news. An Islamic terrorist group claims responsibility for the attack.

Adapting to the mountain habitat is difficult. The fact is, we don't get acclimatized despite the good equipment and provisions we carry. The townsfolk help us. Later we will discover that they also spread the word of our movements. One day, on a trip in search of the remains of an excavation carried out prior to our own, we cross paths with some young Sub-Saharan men. They say they're participating in *Immigration: The Contest*. And I remember having seen programs with that title on TV some time ago in the country formerly known as France, although I only watch la *chaîne d'Art*. I like the discussions with artists and thinkers, like that interview of an expat Spanish writer who claimed that wealthy communities are always inclusive. That societies only become intolerant once they start getting poor, in fear of losing what little wealth they have left.

73

The Sub-Saharans are astonished that the majority of us are European. They are especially astonished that I consider myself European in spite of my skin color. I instantly think of my mother. Then I think of that tiny group of *Homo sapiens* who decided to take the risk of crossing the Red Sea in search of a better place to live.

Based on the stories they tell me of an island chock-full of riches and delights that they tell me, I deduce that these young men are unaware of the reality of the newly re-established European Union. I remember that, at that instant, I thought I wouldn't live on that supposed island for anything in the world. I'm a researcher, I'm skeptical by nature. I am moved by scientific hypotheses, not by illusions. Who would've thought I'd end up living so close to that place. While we converse with the Sub-Saharans, some police agents approach. They behave with absolute courtesy. Then they accompany us to our campsite.

Unfortunately, at the end of the summer there is an ever-dwindling number of police in the mountains. I'm not entirely sure why. One day, when it's been weeks since we've seen a patrol, a terrible storm hits. Everything is flooded. When it clears up, we are surrounded by guys wearing turbans. It's as if they came out of nowhere. I immediately understand that they are Islamic terrorists. They've come to kidnap us.

The following days are like hell. They take us to their camp. First, they separate us. We can't communicate with each other. Then they torture my companions. They shove them in a well and throw stones at them. They pull them out and keep torturing them. I hear their screams in the middle of the night, along with threats in Arabic. I miss Euclides: his touches, his words. I fear for him. I also fear for my life. The next day they take us to their leader. He has a long beard and he wears a white tunic. He preaches a sermon at us in French. He brands us as infidels. He says we are invading sacred lands with our devices and our excavations. I feel

74

the urge to answer that we are looking for proof that all us humans come from the same species. That clashes between beliefs or cultures are stupid. That we are all the same thing. But, in the end, I keep it to myself and say nothing. I relive my childhood fears. His appearance deeply frightens me. So does the look of my companions. They're haggard after the previous night's tortures. They're barefoot. They've torn out their fingernails. One of them has had his finger cut off, and Euclides is missing a strip of skin from his face. Then, the guy with the beard and the white tunic issues his sentence: he condemns us to death in the same way they condemned the young women to death in the city formerly known as Algiers. One of those young women was his daughter. A tear runs down his gaunt face. I am terrified and my eyes dart around, looking for my labmate. There's no time for anything else. Then they take us to the tents in which we were separated the day before. At night, the torture continues. The screams send chills down my spine. The next morning, they lead us out of the camp. They take us, hands tied and at gunpoint, toward some large transports. The look of my companions is heartbreaking. They are swollen and covered in wounds. They've shaved their heads and they all look like monsters. Even Euclides. We travel in the transports for a couple of hours until we reach a village in the mountains. I can't stop crying throughout the journey as I stroke my labmate's head. I try to hug him in spite of the ropes that bind us. The village is a filthy little settlement whose women and children come out to receive us with shrieks. I'm so afraid, I don't notice things I will later discover. The inhabitants are not outraged by my companions' wounds, so I suppose it's not the first time they've seen something like this. What happens next is Dantesque. They pull us down from the transports, but I'm the only one they untie. They've prepared a more terrible end for me. The leader recites a few words in Arabic that I understand. I know they are part of a prayer, although they are heavy with imperative messages. They've erected a platform and they lift us all up onto it. I am forced to watch up close as they douse my companions with gasoline one by one. Then they set them on fire. They all scream. I'm less than two meters away. I am stunned by their shrieks of agony. I make out the suffocating odor of death. They grab me by the nape of my neck and force me to witness the death throes of my friends in the flames. They record everything with a video camera so they can later post it on YouTube. I get dizzy. I vomit. When they set fire to Euclides, I lose consciousness. I wake up in a dark room. It seems I've spent the whole day sleeping, although I feel as if I've only had my eyes closed for five minutes since seeing Euclides burn. The leader of the terrorists tells me they are not done with me yet. He shaves my head. He orders two of his men to take me out of there and carry me to another tent. I fear the worst, so they have to force me. They have to drag me. Fear drives me to fight back, to try to survive. I scream, but I am surrounded only by silence and the accusatory gazes of the women shielded behind their veils. They pull me into a room. They leave me in the dark. Soon, the figure of the leader appears. I make out his white tunic and long beard across the threshold. He is joined by two gunmen. They give off a strong odor. I remember my dead companions. I feel nauseous. The leader jumps on top of me and loudly tears at my clothes. I want to scream, but after all that's happened I have no willpower. He touches me. He grabs me. He shaves off my pubic hair. He bites me all over my body. His henchmen laugh. I'm disgusted, ashamed. I feel disgusted by my own body. And a vertigo I've never felt before...

Let me spare you the details. I'll only say that, after the guy walks out the door, the young woman I met in the hammam appears. She tells me she's my sister, she's seen my ID document. Then everything is revealed. The man who raped me is my own father. They've known about our expedition since I left the hammam.

76

They found out about our presence through Amina. She is behind all this. They've decided to take vicarious revenge for the repression of the police by punishing us, simply because we don't think like them. I am the living example of what happens if you stray from their path. Later I will find out that my father destroys the only papers that identify me; this will lead to the second half of my problems. At any rate, they let me live.

The fact is, over the next few days, my sister tries to get closer to me. She also speaks of this supposedly marvellous island in the middle of the Mediterranean. I don't know who could've told her all this rubbish. I don't believe a word she says. I remember Euclides' body burning. I ask her if what has happened to me is what she wants for all women who don't think like her. Unsurprisingly, the only answer I get is silence. One day I go outside, because they've finally agreed to untie me, and I find myself faced with a terrifying scene. Two young men on matching camels pass by, one on each side of me. They are identical. One image is the carbon copy of the other. They even seem to keep pace with each other's movements. I run back to the room where I was imprisoned, scared to death. But the next day, I decide to research my surroundings. I find surprising things. The flowers grow in doubles. The two shoots always come out the same size. The houses are also built symmetrically, in pairs. And the few trees that stand before a few of the residences are also planted in pairs, as if one were the photocopy of the other. It's a clear abnormality in nature. During that week, I find out that the goats are normally born twins. And the stray dogs wander around in pairs with the same patches on their flanks. I don't want to ask about agricultural production because I think I know the answer. I know I'm not in Villa Godói. But I'm afraid I'm living in the doppelgänger paradise. I think I already know the reason behind my genetic peculiarities. One night I dream of Zwilling again, but this time my sister is his accomplice. I

77

wake up afraid. A few days later, the man who is supposedly my father comes to tell me I must leave. They lift me onto a transport and put a blindfold over my eyes so I can't remember the path we take. In the end, I get away from that cursed place just like my mother when she fled with me years before. They abandon me at the first provincial city we reach. They give me a few coins and some clothes before they leave. There, I take a public transport and get to the city formerly known as Algiers, after three days' journey. I go to seek shelter at my aunt's house. I explain everything that happened and she takes pity on me. She doesn't ask any questions.

Next, I try to put my legal status in order with the authorities of the newly re-established European Union. I explain the whole story and tell them I formed part of the expedition that sadly disappeared: "The Great Journey of Humanity." I show them my shaved head. At first, they're agreeable. But when they ask me to identify myself and I tell them I've lost my ID document, and the terrorists destroyed my passport, their attitude changes. They become terribly skeptical. Even though my mother applies to reestablish my nationality from the country formerly known as France, they say I don't show up on their computers. One day they send me to another office, from there they send me to the building across the street, an old colonial-style apartment block where they end up sending me back to the first office. I get desperate. A customs official says I shouldn't complain so much, I'm the one to blame for the situation. And so I start the only process still possible for me. I try to request political asylum. As I understand it, I have sufficient reasons to do so. I've been raped by the leader of an Islamist group, my companions have been burned alive, and my life is in danger if I stay in the country formerly known as Algeria. But, in the office of the European Union, they tell me they process hundreds of thousands of requests for asylum every year, and they think mine doesn't stand much of a chance. They send me to some other departments. They

78

treat me with scorn, as if they thought I was lying. The next day, an official explains that the only remaining possibility for me to get my life back in Europe is to try out for one of the editions of *Immigration: The Contest*. It seems unbelievable. Having to participate in a contest just to recover something that's mine. *Mon Dieu!* But I don't doubt their words, and I leave my aunt's house behind to go and try out. Thanks to my excellent French and my considerable level of Spanish and English, which I learned in school, they don't make me pass an extra challenge like the others.

The program doesn't go badly for me in the first couple of weeks. My confessional is impeccable. I know the values of French society and the advantages of the Francophone community inside out, and this is clear in my first statement. Nonetheless, from the third week on, I start to notice a sense of rejection from the audience. Some viewers say there are already too many people like me where they live, with the same skin color and similar eyes. I try to defend myself and I talk about the rape. About my childhood in the country formerly known as France. About my studies. About my European nationality. I also explain that we all come from the same species. That our traits have simply changed over the course of centuries. That, at first, we all had dark skin. That white skin is an anomaly caused by cold and the need for Vitamin D. And I explain that dark skin is not as well equipped to produce Vitamin D in climates with little sunlight. This affects the bones and, as a consequence, the pelvis of women with dark skin, who find it more difficult to give birth. I conclude by affirming that natural selection places light skin ahead of dark skin in cold climates. Nonetheless, many people don't believe me. I speak with the program's organizers. They give me a list of nearby editions of the contest in other languages. I choose an edition in Spanish that takes place on a small island, given my skill level in that language. This is how I show up by surprise. I had no idea I was going to find my sister among the contestants who meet me at the port of The Island. But I'm far from excited about the reunion. I have no faith in her terrorist ideas. For her part, she's scared to death. She doesn't know where to look on the day of my arrival. The same thing happens to the Minister of Immigration when we meet. She is none other than one of the twins who made fun of me in school, even though they earned lower grades than me in all our classes. The daughter of the winner of the elections that changed the course of history, who argued that immigrants should live in concentration camps. I ask her about her sister, that pale little girl who sat in class with me. She doesn't know what to say. Strangely, I see on her skin the symbol my sister and I share, tattooed on her left forearm: II. I'd never noticed it before.

The night of my arrival, there's a special episode. We hear a few fragments of the first confessional from the young man we all call the Kid. I agree completely with what he says about Western society. He talks about the impossibility of women and homosexuals living in societies as savage as the one represented by my father and my sister. What's more, he speaks excellent Spanish. The fact is, I agree so strongly that, after hearing his words, I assume he will be the favorite. I understand I must take care to act in my own interests. Especially after the police checkpoint challenge. I hate it because it reminds me of my first trip to Europe, and I have to compete in a state of nervousness and doubt. I let the other contestants get away when I should have held them prisoner. My sister, on the other hand, sets about cuffing them and throwing them into the fenced enclosure. We don't seem to have the same blood in our veins.

I recognize that the Kid is the person I most appreciate on the inside, even to the point of considering him my friend. But he's also the only one who could cast a shadow over my chances of winning the contest. I know how the European audience thinks. They want to hear a speech that puts them in a good light, and only the Kid or I could articulate that. And he gives off a fragility that gives him an advantage. This fragility seems to be the cause of his sudden illness. Nevertheless, it doesn't keep him from pulling himself together weeks later, which greatly surprises me. When he gets sick, I think the malnutrition he must have suffered in his childhood will prevent his swift recovery. But I'm wrong.

When he's back in shape, we have to get through the greenhouse challenge together. The fact is, I'm not cut out for picking eggplants as is demanded of us by the contest's rules. The Kid and I lose the challenge and earn ourselves a week of hunger; a hunger intensified by the exhaustion built up in the hot bed challenge, in which my performance leaves much to be desired. The day they end the challenge, I'm exhausted and it's hard for me to pay attention. I normally sleep eight hours a day, and the interruptions to my routine put me in a bad mood. They keep me from performing on a solid level. Dead tired while the Kid sleeps peacefully on his cot after he wins, I come face to face with my sister at the bedroom door. The continuous hardships I've suffered since I arrived at this edition end up weakening my patience. What's more, all the circumstances surrounding the Kid's poisoning dry up what little trust I had in my sister. I lose consciousness in the middle of the argument. When I come to, they're about to throw Amina out of the contest due to the audience's disapproval. Based on what they've seen on the screen, they think she's the top suspect behind the poisoning. I think it's poetic justice. Unfortunately, she gets away with it, I'm not sure how.

The fact is, the time has come for the audience to make a decision, since we've reached the final special. I suppose, due to my scientific knowledge, I would be the most productive for European society, in which I was already integrated. But I also know the audience tends to let itself get carried away by emotions, and maybe they'll choose the Kid. In any case, now the decision is in your hands. 五

81

What impressed me most about a statement as full of surprises as Ánima's was the story of the "great journey of humanity." There were so many parallels with past narratives of the promised land that it scared me a little. It occured to me that the biblical tale of Moses or the legend that Virgil created around Aeneas may have been inspired by that journey after centuries and centuries of oral transmission. Of course, when I try to imagine who or what could have convinced those hominids to risk their lives and cross the Red Sea, the first thing that comes to mind is the power of a story. Only a powerful story of the existence of a rich, fertile land over the horizon, a land that could alleviate their material hardships, would be able to convince those beings to overcome their survival instinct and risk the lives of every member of their tribe.

It became evident that Ánima idealized everything related to the "great journey of humanity," although, after hearing her story, it was understandable that she would do so in order to honor her own epic journey, and her mother's. What's more, when you listened to her talk you saw her as a purebred European even though she was born in Africa. Writing out her words has been by far my easiest project up to now.

Nonetheless, in spite of its beauty, it didn't seem that the idyllic tale of the world's first migration put forth by Ánima could be applied now. In the end, during her speech, I imagined what would happen to that same tribe in our times, with its borders, drones, walls, and *Immi-*

gration challenges, and I didn't much like their odds. Especially with people like the Minister directing European politics. A person who, two weeks ago, confessed to me that it was impossible to govern a country in which more than ten percent of the inhabitants were immigrants with no right to vote. They were people who, according to her, eroded national identity, something so necessary for the solidarity and governability of a State. That's why she always appealed in her speeches to the fear that foreign groups might impose their political agenda, and to the danger of the disappearance of European culture; a culture that, according to what we had discovered from Ánima, had not interested her much in her teenage years, even if she now boasted that she had been listening to Mozart her whole life.

The Minister's totalitarian discourse has sunk in with ease among the voters on the lowest social strata. And it has met with no response from more educated groups, those capable of undertaking a more complex analysis of the circumstances but more interested in our own selfish matters, like my ex-girlfriend and myself.

In the end, it's impossible to forget the images of short-lived rafts crammed full of passengers heading for the Old Continent. These scenes sent a fright through European public opinion. But if you compare them to the seventeenth-century texts that told of the arrival of splendid merchant ships, equally crammed, but this time with raw materials ready for trade, extracted from distant lands and received with open arms, you can't help but let slip an ironic smile. One image was the negative of the other. As it happens, the fortune of the Minister's family came from her great-grandfather, who had gotten rich in the army defending the colonial interests of the country formerly known as France.

Contradictions dominated the Minister's actions just as they did her thoughts. Ultimately, she was unable to help Ánima come back to her after so many years. She could have testified about her origin, but she didn't. On the contrary, she supported Amina as much as necessary. Not only did she come to her aid in the case of the first confessional, she also helped her at another key moment, reminding the audience of her success in the police checkpoint challenge during the special when they wanted to eliminate her since she was suspected of the Kid's poisoning.

The police checkpoint challenge was a role-playing activity. The participants had to alternate between posing as border police and illegal immigrants hoping to get into Europe. Those who acted as police had to return the immigrants to the other side of the wire fence by force, as quick as they could. Based on the way these new apprentice police officers acted—the way they carried out the pat down, how thoroughly they interrogated, and, above all, their attitude—the audience evaluated the contestants' level of commitment to the recently re-established Union.

Amina clearly performed best in the challenge. Nonetheless, it didn't make much sense to bring that up at the moment when the public wanted to eliminate her for other reasons. It was hard to understand the Minister's unconditional support, unless it came down to the fact that the presence of characters like Amina in Europe justifies the votes she receives. In the end, she's a controversial person all around; the same person who, in her first visit to the contest, when she wasn't yet a minister, could have single-handedly caused the the program to disappear from the TV guide, despite the fact that she's now our biggest contributor. Good thing we had Vladimir Lazarovich, Silvio Pérez's right hand man.

Lazarovich was our lead producer; a Russian multi-millionaire who loved working in media. He had gained a lot of experience putting on musical shows for Russian television, jam packed with dance numbers and scantily clad young ladies. He went from director to producer and then to manager, always in connivance with the Russian regime. Until, one day, he decided to move to Europe. At first, he wasn't keen on the idea of becoming a citizen of the newly re-established European Union, as he unequivocally confirmed. Yet, with the passage

85

of time, the rich Russians who resided in other countries started to think it was rather distinguished to become nationalized Europeans or citizens of the O.N.A.N. Lazarovich says he decided to take European citizenship the day he found out that Roman Abramovich II, the son of Roman Abramovich I and his main competitor, had become European. After that, he had little time to get rid of what was, for him, a ridiculous quantity of money, and to get hold of a passport from the newly re-established European Union. He did so thanks to the investment-based residency program that was offered in Europe. Logically, Lazarovich invested in the audiovisual world. This allowed him to become the principal partner of Silvio Pérez. The whole operation took place with the support of the Minister's family, which had maintained excellent relations with the Russian elite for years.

That connection was a miracle for the contest's chance at survival, since the reason behind the first visit from the Minister of Integration, then the future Minister, was that she was on her pre-campaign. She appeared off the shores of The Island on her private ship: a luxury yacht. She wanted to speak with the contestants, to convince then that there was no space for them in the newly re-established European Union. She brought a placard to announce it. A boldfaced message with a patina of provisionality that seemed to suggest so many future benefits. Curiously, she came along with her closest supporters and the most important media players from the channels that competed with Silvio Pérez, who had arrived on The Island on the same ship.

Those of us who worked on the program couldn't allow her to access the facility because her visit was not planned. We were always collaborating with politicians, even more so than with the media because, among other reasons, some politicians are in the pockets of Silvio Pérez. Nonetheless, it became evident that the trip was an initiative on the then-future Minister's part to advance her career in her party, as was clear from the feigned grimace of concern she flashed only when the cameras zoomed in on her.

The then-future Minister was willing to camp out at the doors of the contest facility until we let her in. This was terrible publicity for the program. But, given our isolation, we didn't know it until our news colleagues from one of Silvio Pérez's channels put us on notice. If the audience saw fit, we would have to cancel the whole season. The upcoming elections and the reordering of the political scene might be placing the model offered by *Immigration* in doubt, along with many jobs, including my own. So we asked Vladimir Lazarovich to act. Our technical director spoke in person with the then-future Minister. After their conversation, he allowed us to override our protocol and let her in. And so, she entered the contest's set and spoke with the finalists in a scene that flipped Europe on its head. It was nothing otherworldly, really. The then-future Minister sat down in the campsite, in front of the contestants, and tried to convince them that the newly re-established European Union could only take in the winner of each season; with this, the new actress on the political scene meant she wanted the existing filters on the flow of immigration to remain as they were. Nonetheless, she couldn't avoid putting on a little political theatre. She argued that, if the rest of the participants also meant to enter, they would become parasites, sucking on our economy, not taking into account that sometimes the show's organization itself created other editions on sets unknown to us in order to fill the quotas; she waited to say these words around the central campfire, with the flames fearfully illuminating her face. The camera also focused on the contestants, one by one. They behaved calmly. We had forced them all to sign a document in which they promised to demand nothing if they didn't win in order to avoid future legal problems, so they were more than prepared to take in her words.

In actual fact, the then-future Minister's party had reached an agreement with Silvio Pérez on the quotas determined by that year's editions. But this was no obstacle; the controversy that was generated would lead to a good result for her in the elections that would take

87

place months later, and the same controversy would be the reason behind her appointment as Minister of Integration at the young age of twenty-seven. Since then, she has always been involved in our contest, to the extent that she is now the one who supervises the fence-jump challenge in the city that is no longer known as Melilla. But Silvio Pérez was still concerned to see someone capable of an act of public treason out of pure self-interest at the height of power. And so, I cooperated with the Minister at my boss's request, and I showed her all my writings related to the program. As it happens, I designed the outline of the greenhouse challenge with her.

The challenge involved harvesting as many eggplants as possible in the greenhouse we had built for the occasion beside the camp. They had to pick them with their mouths, just to add pathos. We divided the participants into two teams. On one side, Amina and Mamadou. On the other, the Kid and Ánima. We planned to provide extra food, a box of matches, and some sunscreen to whichever team was proclaimed the winner. All of us on the crew had to stay on our toes in order to catch the altercations that, what with the physical effort and the heat inside the greenhouse, would be generated within each pair. Especially between the losers, who would have to adjust their food rations for a week.

It was clear that Mamadou's team was going to win. Ánima showed herself to be an intellectual capable of weaving an idyllic tale about the migratory nature of humanity, but not so capable of frantically bending up and down to pick eggplants with her mouth. The Kid wasn't so lucky in the challenge either, but he was finally over his convalescence, that's for sure.

On the other hand, it's worth recognizing that the Kid's story had allowed me to recover the African heritage I received from my father, along with his physical traits. The fact is, my parent's stories, those tales with which he hoped to preserve my grandmother's memory, had left me deeply ashamed. Especially at the moment of my life when

88

I was beginning to get over my adolescence and I started to vanquish my complexes, which coincided with the time when he was trying to impose the most absolute of patriarchies over my mother and me. I was already going out with plenty of markedly masculine young women, more than a little postmodern, more than a little transgressive. That made my father nervous because he had always wanted me to be a traditional girl. Soon my parents divorced and I grew even more distant from them. I isolated myself from the cultural values he wanted to pass down to me. Maybe I've tried to hide it until now. I've always wanted to be as European as possible. I preferred science fiction and robot stories to my father's tales. That was one of the reasons for my move to Germany; my desire to be European, my mother's rejection of my sexuality, since behind her liberal image she revealed herself to be just as authoritarian as my father; and my breakup with my first girl-friend. Nonetheless, it is thanks to my African heritage that, in the end, I've been able to process the tale I've heard again tonight: the story of Mamadou, which will explain your last unanswered questions. He had a lot to say in his final confessional. He wove a story riddled with voices from different corners of Africa and Europe: proof that more than a few paths are trodden beyond the Strait and the set of *Immigration.* ⊞

REPUBLIQUE DE COTE D'IVOIRE

Name: Mamadou

Age: 20

Skin color: black

Eye color: black

Hair color: black

Profession: trader

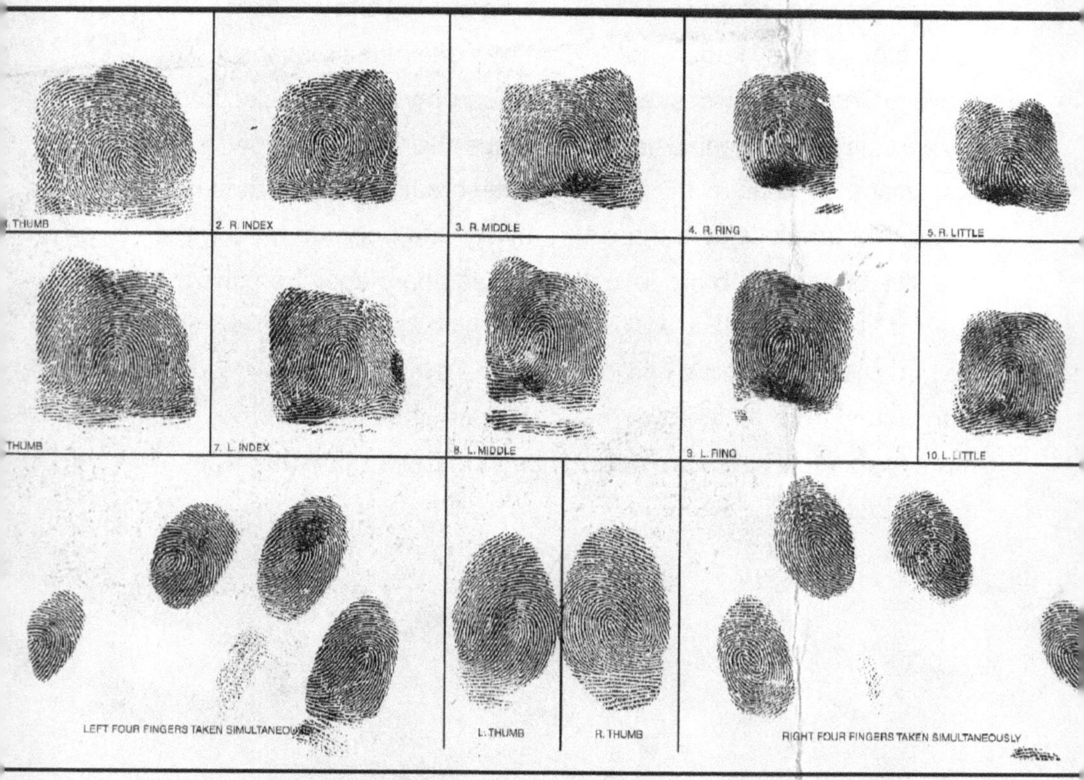

1. THUMB	2. R. INDEX	3. R. MIDDLE	4. R. RING	5. R. LITTLE
THUMB	7. L. INDEX	8. L. MIDDLE	9. L. RING	10. L. LITTLE

LEFT FOUR FINGERS TAKEN SIMULTANEOUSLY

L. THUMB | R. THUMB

RIGHT FOUR FINGERS TAKEN SIMULTANEOUSLY

Sign--

The Chosen One

MAMADOU WILL SPEAK OF THE STORY of those who reached Europe from the bowels of Africa, prisoners of misery and desperation. He will speak of himself, of the chosen one. He will speak of war, of enemy troops drawing close to his city to raze it to the ground. And of the farewell, of his mother washing the door of their house so he could journey with cool winds, and of the amulet she gave him just before he left while the shadows of his fate were reflected off that wet sand.

He will speak of the escape from Shangana, the country once known as the Ivory Coast. A difficult journey for the chosen one when he does not yet know what he is, and he has to jump onto the first truck he can find after paying the driver; his eyes tearful and his clothes soaked through with a terrible odor. Twenty hours surrounded by onions to sneak through the checkpoints of the enemy army and reach the city known in the old days as Bojaria, on the edge of the desert. The place from which you can reach the city of desire, known in the old days as Dorothea, the crossroads where the true journey would begin.

In Bojaria the chosen one discovers the nature of man: ungrateful when it comes to paying for his work, whether it be sowing seeds in the fields, collecting metal, or cleaning houses; generous when he knows suffering, as in the case of that group of athletes, the group of soccer players. Eleven young men who confront their rivals with a single leg each, thanks to a pair of crutch-

91

es and the strength of their arms; young men he had met in the hospital, sharing the terrible fate implied by an amputated leg, until they decided to band together into the team that triumphed in the soccer tournament of the city known in the old days as Bojaria, thanks to the teamwork that made up for what they lacked. They explain that they have lost their legs on the way to the city known in the old days as Dorothea, in the minefield that stretches across the path between the two towns. Then the chosen one fears that he will fail, he also sees his leg amputated. He does not know whether to continue the journey or try to survive in the city known in the old days as Bojaria, not changing his luck but at least holding on to his two lower extremities. He knows he cannot go back to his family, since the troops of the enemy army have already invaded all of Shangana, the country once known as the Ivory Coast, and they will keep him from retracing his steps. He decides to look for work. He puts himself at the service of a policeman. Together they patrol the streets and confiscate the goods of all the immigrants who pass through the city; men who arrive in the same conditions in which the chosen one arrived, and whose pockets he now empties.

The guard is shortsighted and old. One day the chosen one tries to keep a part of their earnings in the hopes of saving up for his journey to the city known in the old days as Dorothea. He also does this to make up for the policeman's abuses: the continuous groping and the hot breath on his neck at night. But he fails spectacularly because the guard's hearing is so acute that, when the two metal pieces fall into the waist pouch of he who speaks and start to clink, his boss wants to know the source of this clinking, he grabs him by the neck and forces him to give them back. Then he gives him a beating, reminding him who feeds him—although he feeds him very little—and gives him shelter in his house, if a mat two fingers thick laid out on a patio, barely protected from the

92

rain by a canopy, with a well in the center to provide water, can be called shelter. To avoid more blows, he who speaks hides only one coin per day from then on.

The chosen one does not know if his luck will ever change. He has lost the hope of traveling to the city known in the old days as Dorothea. He only wishes to buy his freedom with what little wealth he has. But one day he meets Cissé, a young man from Teranga, the country once known as Senegal; the policeman wants to rob the young man, but he buys his freedom in exchange for a scrap of food, which he hands over to them.

Cissé had abandoned his village because the fish had disappeared from the coasts of Teranga, and in their place the pirates had appeared. They were former fishermen who, to feed their families, now attacked the big, white, silent ships that had stolen their food with their new ways of taking from the sea. It was easy to keep up with the movements of the ghost ships on that ocean of sadness, to later strike and take their crew prisoner until their bosses or their families paid for their freedom. But Cissé didn't want to start that life because he saw how the bosses were corrupted and, when they started out making sure the ransom helped to feed the whole village, they ended up getting rich for themselves and letting their people die of hunger. That is why he preferred to travel to Europe. He let himself be carried away by the siren song that told of *Immigration: The Contest*, of how easy it was to participate and win. His optimism did the rest. He sold his satellite dish, as well as his small business where he carved utensils out of wood, and he set off toward the north.

Cissé is the first to tell the chosen one of the contest. He explains that it is the only safe way to reach the city known in the old days as Dorothea. He also tells him of The Island of the Good Year, where you can eat the sweetest things and drink the most exotic drinks. You are even free to enjoy what few women live on

The Island, which is seen live on television sets all over Europe. This convinces the chosen one that he must make it to the very end. But the journey has many difficulties, Cissé has already tried it twice. He explains that, out of every five candidates, only one gets through the qualifying challenge, but he who speaks is not scared this time.

That night the chosen one rises stealthily from his mat and approaches the hollow where he stores his coins. He knows that any noise could wake up his boss. But he has insured his escape. In case the policeman hears something and gets up, guided by his extraordinary sense of hearing, he has tied a cord to the door that opens onto the patio where he sleeps. At the other end of the string he places a pouch with two coins that, if all goes well, will clink at just the right spot if the guard opens the door to follow the steps of he who speaks. This is what happens that morning. But, while the chosen one approaches freedom, his pursuer approaches the opening at the center of the courtyard where the pouch with the two metal pieces is hanging. His boss's bad eyesight does the rest. He does not see the bricks that encircle the well, nor the hole that opens into the center of the earth; he only allows himself to be guided by his hearing and, as he moves toward the source of the clinking, he plunges into the darkness of the well.

The chosen one walks away happy as he hears the groans of the guard, who demands that he help him climb out. Nonetheless, the young man remembers the hardships he made him suffer, the abuses and the tight spots. From a distance, he answers that in the well he can drink all the water he wants, he just needs to reach the two coins and buy some food to eat. "Be at peace!" he cries to him, and then he leaves. He meets up with Cissé and other young men like him who are waiting on the outskirts of the city known in the old days as Bojaria. They set off together for the train station, where anyone who signs up for the challenge can be considered as a candidate, although no one keeps count of all the hopefuls who build up on the outskirts of the city.

Far away, by the station, he makes them out: the ancient electric trains that only work in Africa, even though in some places there are no longer cables and they have been replaced by transports. The challenge is clearly governed by strict rules that the chosen one knows thanks to Cissé's explanations. He prepares himself with the rest of the participants. First he prays, then he kneels and places his hands against his legs. Before that, he has tucked the pouch of coins into an interior pocket, from which he will not remove it for a long time. Then he hears the first whistle, deep in the middle of the African night; he stands up straight and holds on with the tips of his fingers and toes. When the second whistle sounds, he is prepared, his legs tense but ready to spring into action. First he feels the unease among the participants when the train starts to move. A couple of young men also move, and they are immediately eliminated at the hands of the watchmen, who supervise to ensure the challenge goes correctly. The chosen one does not move. He knows he must wait for the third whistle, which means the train is in motion, and then there is nothing the watchmen can do. Cissé has explained it to him. He squeezes his mother's talisman in his right hand and holds on with courage until that moment. When he hears it, he is off like a shot. He has to transmit as much speed as possible to his legs because the train already seems to grow distant over the horizon. But his training in his native Shangana takes effect. The distance starts to grow shorter, even as the outline of the train becomes blurry down the track. He is the first to reach the wagon and cling on to its doors. He feels like a hero. In an instant, Cissé is by his side.

It is hard to bear the bitter cold on the outside of the train toward the city known in the old days as Dorothea. On its roof travel the chosen one, his friend Cissé, and a boy called Musa. He is a young man who has fled from a war in the opposite direction to the one suffered by he who speaks; a war in which foreign troops are invading the country of Shangana's attackers for religious reasons.

After a long journey, they reach the gates of the city known in the old days as Dorothea. They say four aluminum towers rise from the city's walls, flanking seven gates with spring-loaded drawbridges that span the moat, whose water feeds into four green canals that cross the city and divide it into nine neighborhoods, each one with three hundred houses and seven hundred chimneys. Now they could tell that the desert surrounds it, and also that its inhabitants are surprised by the influence it exercises over the travelers, who come with the intention of spending a few days there and end up staying longer against their will.

It is no tall tale: more than one city known in the old days as Dorothea exists on the borders of the Sahara, they appear and disappear even though they are one and the same city. They say the Dorothea where the chosen one arrives is the meeting point for those who come from the south and those who come from the east, and in its markets you can buy the most varied things. But maybe it is more important to say that its streets fork down unsuspected paths, and that its women are very good looking, although they always keep their faces covered. In his desire to possess them, one believes he is enjoying the city even when he is its slave. Something similar ends up happening to the chosen one. For several days he walks through the market, searching for someone to guide him to the other side of the desert, to The Island of the Good Year, hoping they will not ask for too much money to do so. But he discovers the amount the contest intermediaries require in order to register him for the challenge that could authorize him to cross the desert and access the next phase is very high; he starts looking for a job that would allow him to pay this amount, as he plans to save the money he earned in the city known in the old days

96

as Bojaria for The Island of the Good Year; until one morning he lays eyes on a young woman with dark skin and almond-shaped eyes who crosses his path toward the gate of the souk. The young woman takes off her veil and shows him a sensual mouth and a perfect nose, along with the beautiful eyes he has already seen. He falls to his knees before her beauty. She confuses him for one of the boys who work in the market, and she says to him, "Oh, errand boy! Grab the basket and follow me." She speaks in a strange way in a strange language, which he will have to translate because it was nothing like Spanish. The chosen one decides to follow her. He goes after her after picking up the basket that was dropped on the ground, leading to the girl's mistake.

The young woman buys the most varied products from the market's most exotic stalls. The chosen one carries the goods to the door of the house she points out. When he goes inside, he finds out she does not live alone, but with another girl, even more beautiful than the first, which gives the chosen one a great desire to stay and live in these lodgings. That is his intention, but he does not know how to say it. He expresses himself in a confusing way in that strange language that the young women speak. He who speaks can hardly translate it. The chosen one says: "You live in the solitude of this great house and there is no man to keep you company; your swaying waists show that you are the perfect instruments for the most beautiful chords of the body, but a chord can never make harmony if it does not combine three instruments: the harp, the zither, and the flute. You have only two and you need a third, which is none other than the flute. I will be your flute and I will act as a well mannered man, capable of conducting this business!" Words answered by the girl who had been in the house when the chosen one arrived; she answered in that strange language in which they expressed themselves: "Oh, errand boy! Don't you know that we're virgins? That it is through our bodies that we obtain the goods that let us survive at this crossroads? We don't want men with whom to share these earnings, as it is well known that men are idle and like to take advantage of the body and the work of a woman."

He who speaks does not know how to translate what came next, so he will say that, upon replying, the chosen one engaged in an elevated dialogue with the girls. As this happened, they heard loud knocks on the door. The young woman whom the chosen one had met in the market went to open it; she came back announcing that in the house's threshold were two one-eyed foreigners with shaved heads. Again, she expressed herself strangely and said: "Our bellies are going to get nice and full tonight because these foreigners come with pockets crammed with money and a terrible thirst to quench." In spite of the chosen one's opposition, the elder girl told them to come in.

The foreigners penetrated the house, eager to share out the loot of those womanly bodies, until they met the gaze of the chosen one, which told them the situation had grown more complicated. They had to organize a tie breaker to decide who was not going to sleep warm that night. They agreed that each would tell his story; the most boring tale would go without a prize. Since the two foreigners were each missing their left eye and had shaved heads, which was already exotic, the young women decided they would be the first to speak.

So, the first of the one-eyed men, a tall man with matte black skin, stepped forward to tell his story. He also spoke in that strange language, as it seemed that everyone did in the city known in the old days as Dorothea. He who speaks hopes he can tell the story accurately. I think he said: I am going to tell you the reason why I lost my eye, why I shaved off my hair, and the reason for my presence in this city. If I am one-eyed, I am to blame, and my shaved head has a great deal to do with it.

98

I come from Aksum, once known as Ethiopia, where a civil war has devastated the country for years. Two days after they murdered my father, I decided to leave my city behind. I reached the border, ever more dangerous; there I lived for a few years in a refugee camp. I also heard, from the mouths of my countrymen, that some European countries were especially sensitive to tragedies like the one we were suffering in Aksum. They spoke to me of countries then known as Germany, Sweden, and Norway. They all seemed like paradises compared to my native land, where so much blood was spilled and so many executions took place, like my father's. It didn't take me long to join together with three other guys, leave the camp, and reach the capital of Swahiland, which was Kenya back then. Our plan was to show up at the first embassy we could find of any one of these nations. We first requested asylum from the country then known as Germany. A few weeks later we received the response at the makeshift camp where we lived on the outskirts of the city then known as Nairobi. We got lucky. The country then known as Germany had not yet reduced their asylum quota, as they would later. All but one of us, a young man with a criminal record for robbery, received a refugee card and a plane ticket to leave within a week for Germany.

The first few days in my new country were terrible. No one had told me how cold it was. That was not the promised land. Luckily, I managed to find a place in a refugee shelter, and little by little I made contact with other countrymen, since many of us were displaced by the war to the country then known as Germany. After a few months, I was already sharing a living space with ten other Africans: a run-down apartment in the slums of the city then known as Hamburg. They put up all of us asylum seekers in poor areas, which didn't please their residents, since they thought their government was giving us goods that they lacked; arguments and confrontations were common, and since I always avoid disputes

99

and try to do good to my fellow man, I didn't spend much time around the neighbors.

One day, one of my countrymen told me of the pleasures of German nightlife; of the nightclubs and the way the local girls welcomed foreigners, which was very different from how our neighbors welcomed us. At the time I was good looking and I had a good mane growing because I'm a Rasta. I wasn't short on chances to start deep relationships with German girls, although I must say the competition with other immigrants was ferocious; that's why I sank into the world of drugs.

I discovered that those girls who liked the cold German night, the most appealing, the best looking, the most daring, and, why not, the richest, were into a very specific kind of immigrant, those they considered dangerous. I also discovered that my simple and flexible nature made them not so interested in me. They went around with dangerous guys who mistreated them in public. Once I understood that, I didn't take long to start working as a drug dealer. It wasn't because of my economic situation, as some believe, since my work as a trash collector, given to me by the German state, along with social support and my calm and thrifty ways, was enough to survive.

I teamed up with a local dealer, helping him move his product. But I had to quit my job because I needed an air of danger that the garbage truck and the uniform couldn't provide. Luckily, the drugs led me to what I wanted: to ride the most beautiful women, women I never would have tasted before, to delight in their backsides, their exquisite vulvas, in exchange for some lines in a discotheque, some pills in a club, or my simple presence as a representative of the drug business, which attracted them in itself. That was how I met Marliz, a German girl with skin pale as snow and hair black as crow's feathers. I fell in love with her instantly. I met her one night along with a friend of hers called Ingrid, a somewhat stuck-up young woman who, luckily, soon left us alone. I was already a little tired of my own insecurities and of so many relationships taking place in a single night. I thought I should settle down, and Marliz seemed to be the right person for me. I took advantage of the fact that she wanted to pass herself off as a woman of the world in the local nightlife spot known back then as St. Pauli in order to make her mine. Against my will, I had to pretend to be an even more dangerous man so as not to lose her. Many men prowled around her, and I wasn't willing to mistreat her, because my religion obliges me to respect women. So I had to set a trap for my partner and take over the drug trade in the spots we controlled for myself. I informed the guards one day when I knew he would bring a car full of goods; they arrested him on the spot.

Within a few months, my Rasta image and my ample centimeters allowed me to extend my power throughout St. Pauli. While this was happening, Marliz stayed by my side. But one day I was introduced to Klaus, a young German man who was accompanied by a Russian guy who protected him from any and all danger. They wanted to work with me. Klaus didn't like Africans, or any foreigners, as you will see later. Nonetheless, he needed me in order to do business in the area, and he pitched me a pact with good conditions. I offered him the territory and he distributed the product, which came from North Africa. Unfortunately, he was much more ambitious than I. I've already said that my character is calm and accommodating, that I didn't want to get rich off the drug trade. Klaus did, he wanted more money than his hands could hold. He immediately took an interest in Marliz, but I didn't realize it. For months I thought ambition was the only thing that drove him forward. I should have suspected something the moment Marliz started complaining about how many foreigners lived in her city, up to the point that she claimed they should concentrate them all in the same neighborhood, something I hadn't heard since

101

I moved away from my previous shared apartment to St. Pauli. It was true that more immigrants arrived everyday, nobody knew exactly why.

One day, Klaus's bodyguard, the Russian guy who protected him from all danger, came to see me. I was resting on one of the benches by the side of my house, known as Alter Elbpark; he had found me through my cell phone. First I thought he was coming to betray his boss, to take his place, but his bloodshot eyes told me something else. I was scared, I thought his soul was possessed, that he was a demon who wanted to lead me into temptation. That day I had taken hashish, as my beliefs dictate, and that could have affected me. But my prediction was correct, and the young man confided in me that, thanks to him, I would achieve the most incredible things. I asked him to show me. At that moment, it seemed to me that a pair of wings grew out of his back. Frightening, black wings, hard to the touch, as I would feel afterwards, that proved to me that I was face to face with some sort of genie or demon. He jumped up and started to glide through the sky. He made a complete turn before my eyes, then descended so fast that, when he landed by my side, he seemed out of breath. Strangely, I had the impression that I was the only one who had witnessed his flight. My men looked at Yago, the aerial bodyguard of my partner Klaus, as if nothing had happened. He invited me to hold on to his waist, and I did. In a few seconds we reached the limit of the celestial vault. There I could hear the songs of the descendants of the twelve tribes, as the holy book says. From those heights I looked out at all the people who were spread over the surface of the planet. I saw Africa, my native Africa: the once green fields that had turned ochre; although the helicopters of unidentifiable armies obstructed my view, I could make out long lines of people crossing deserts and gathering at the ports of the continent's coastal cities, trying to climb onto vessels jammed with people. Then I saw the sea, choppy in many places, the waves crashing against the coast of a Europe not yet re-established, and I understood that something terrible was about to happen. That intuition left me shaken. I was afraid for those desperate people who were leaving their villages devoid of youth and I wanted to warn them. Nevertheless, my companion decided we had taken long enough and we descended. But we didn't descend in Africa but rather in the city then known as Hamburg. Sadly, while we plunged toward the ground, I glimpsed a scene I should never have seen. I saw Klaus and Marliz at the door of the mansion he had just bought in the neighborhood then known as Blankenese. He had bought it from the famous leader of a social party in the country then known as Germany, a man named Tony Schröder. Klaus and Marliz kissed, holding hands. I understood that this was Yago's purpose: to reveal the terrible things that were happening, I don't know with what intention. I only know that, as soon as I recognized them, jealousy swept over me. I remember it became hard for me to breathe and I lost consciousness. When I awoke, I was back in Alter Elbpark with Yago. The flying man wanted me to promise that I wouldn't act based on what I had seen. But I forgot my Rastafari principles, paid no heed to his warnings, and set off for Klaus's house, thirsty for vengeance.

My partner had started associating with anti-immigration parties; he was setting himself up as a leader of the local movement against foreigners, so he had told me he didn't want us to see each other so much and he wasn't expecting my visit. As soon as the door opened, I rushed inside. Klaus was standing next to a servant, and, against the precepts of my religion, I leapt on top of him. I was about to strangle him, in spite of his butler's efforts to separate us. When I was about to succeed, Marliz appeared. My hate was so strong that I didn't hear her words. She was saying she had seen me in the neighborhood and decided to follow me. She was claiming she didn't know what I was doing there or why I was attacking my partner. But I wasn't listening. I only noticed the death rattle in Klaus's body. Nevertheless, Marliz grabbed my head and desperately, violently pushed her index finger into my left eye. I suddenly screamed and my hands let go of Klaus's neck. One-eyed as I was at that moment, I built up enough strength for a second attempt and approached my partner, who was lying exhausted on the floor. But the servant held up a cane, threatening me. I had to give up. The worst part was Marliz's words about my condition as a migrant. She remembered little of her interest in me at the bar in that club in the neighborhood then known as St. Pauli, where she tried to make herself pass as a woman of the world. I had become a stranger to her. Humiliated and one-eyed, I fled.

I left there with more hate in me than I had ever felt in my life. This is something my religion punishes. Unable to control myself, I got into the Mercedes that Klaus had bought a few days before and, knowing that a large amount of the product we were selling was in the car, I escaped, not before meeting up with one of my countrymen who tried to cure my injured eye through witchcraft, in vain. I don't have much faith in such rites, but I wasn't going to go to a doctor in my situation. Then I set off on what I thought would be a long journey.

When I stopped to refuel, the guards appeared. I don't know if they followed me, if they knew about Klaus's movements, or if, as I suspect, the aerial Yago had informed them of mine. Their dogs didn't take long to detect the product hidden under the back seats. I wanted to hand over my asylum card, but I had lost it. It had probably fallen off me while I was flying on Yago's shoulders.

The process that followed was typical in such cases: the arrest, the imprisonment, the trial, and, owing to the new laws that were starting to be applied in the country then known as Germany, the repatriation to Aksum, then Ethiopia. It was clear that God had abandoned me due to my evil acts. When I entered the jail, they shaved my head. Since then, I've been shaving it as a sign of penance.

When I returned to my homeland, once again I found a country devastated by war and drought. But it was also a country that produced top quality hashish, and all the bhang on its way to Europe passed through there. In spite of my calm and accommodating nature, I carried on doing business. I entered the service of the local drug-running gangs; I realized that these gangs kept up communication between the different warring groups in each of the States, whether they were Jihadists or Christian militias. I made good deals with a guy called Omar Belmojtar, who moved throughout the Sahel, from Songhai to my dominions, which allowed me to get my hands on very good product. I discovered he was the same contact who supplied Klaus, and that intensified my thirst for vengeance. Back then, Belmojtar had not yet embraced Islam with the fanaticism he would later adopt, but even when he converted he didn't mind doing business with an old Rasta. These groups were the same that supplied the participants of *Immigration: The Contest*. I arrived here, in the city known back then as Dorothea, following the trail that started in the city known back then as Askia. I have no interest in going back to Europe, it's not the promised land. It's more like Babylon. What's more, because of my past and the police reports, I'd probably be left at the gates. Nevertheless, I know there will always be people there who are interested in accumulating treasures and riches like Klaus, and that those people will need product to trade. My purpose is to maintain these relationships, but to supply them with adulterated products, with good form and poor substance, mixing the material with flour and medications. It's my way of taking revenge on Klaus and Marliz. That's why I have traveled day and night toward the city known back then as Dorothea. I suddenly found myself face to face with this one-eyed man and I said to him: I'm a foreigner. He

105

answered: Me too. Then we started talking about how to unload our pent-up anxiety. We started walking together. Luck and fate guided us to this door and we entered your house, where, besides getting all of this off my chest, I hope to make good contacts for both my business and my vengeance, since I know the nature of these establishments and the people who pass through them. That is the reason I lost my eye and I shave my head, and the motive for my presence in this city.

When the first one-eyed man finished his story, the second, a shorter guy than the other, with lighter skin, took a step forward and spoke in the same strange way as the first: I don't want you to think my story holds fewer wonders than my companion's. You should know that I am a man of Songhai, which was called Mali in those times, and that I successfully applied for a tourist visa for the country then known as the Netherlands. It wasn't my preferred destination, but it was the only place that would open the doors of Europe to me. Since, in spite of my education, I had problems in Songhai due to my sympathies toward certain groups, I thought it was time to go. I landed at Charles de Gaulle airport, in the city then known as Paris, and when I was asking around about how to make the connecting flight, I ran into a big group of people. They were followers of a leader who had won the European elections. Then I found out that his xenophobic ideas and the presence of migrants in European cities had launched him toward election. With him were two twin sisters, as beautiful as two moons, and his bodyguards; they were surrounded by a crowd. The rest of his followers awaited him, chanting on the other side of the fence that was meant to be the border. I went along with them and nobody noticed me because the guards were only interested in the leader's safety. In an instant, I was on the other side. The crowd cheered for their leader and I entered the territory of the country then known as France.

Outside the airport, I got in a taxi. I was afraid I would be taken prisoner by the guards and expelled back to my country. The taxi driver scammed me. He charged me a large amount of money, taking advantage of my desperation. I thought nothing of it.

I started looking for work, thinking it would be easy even though I didn't have papers. Nevertheless, the situation got more complicated when the leader I had bumped into at the airport came to power. The neighborhood where I lived was fenced-in and I could hardly get out to look for work. My weariness grew. At that time, verification checkpoints and systematic expulsions were implemented, which could be branded as racism; but in the country then known as France it was a strange, veiled racism. It was a racism that came to life when you stood before an authority and tried to sort out a situation, or when you ran into a pair of guards at the gate in the fence that closed in your neighborhood. Everyone behaved courteously in such situations. Nevertheless, you could tell you were making them uncomfortable. Not just them, but also the witnesses of those scenes. I could tell my stay there was in danger, and I thought I needed a change. I thought the country then known as Spain would be the best place for me.

I arrived in the place that has since ceased to be called Spain after paying 300 euros, which was the common currency in Europe until the numerary system was introduced. It was the same amount I had paid that taxi driver to get away from the airport of the city that has ceased to be called Paris. But this time, my guide, of Spanish origin, took me to my destination with no surprises. He was a cold and distant man, only interested in money. We made the journey at night down a sparsely traveled highway; when I asked the driver where we were, he said we had already been in the country that was my destination for half an hour.

My arrival in the place that was no longer called Spain was difficult. Measures to decrease the number of migrants had also arrived there; there was a lot of tension in the air. At that time, the police asked for your documents on every corner and I didn't speak Spanish, I only spoke English, French, and my native language. Almost nobody spoke those languages, much less the guards, who always forced me to report to the police station. Luckily, I'm a communist, an atheist and a communist, and within two months in the city that is no longer called Barcelona, I learned the language and met an Argentine man who was also an atheist and a communist. We met on the underground transport and made friends. His name was Hernán. That day changed my life: we organized what we started calling a resistance group, which allowed us to often leave the ghetto in which they kept us enclosed. Thanks to these comings and goings, I obtained a temporary permit. My new friend had shaved his head in memory of the victims of Nazism; since his family was Jewish, they had been forced to flee from Europe. To support him, I did the same. From then on, I have kept my head shaved.

With my brand-new permit, and thanks to my friend, I found work in construction. I shared the labor with a very young kid called Mimoun. He was particularly aggressive with women. I warned him I didn't think it was the best attitude to have. He paid me no mind and tried to have sex with the wife of one of our bosses, a blonde with a body of amber and gold. He tried to get with her, and he only managed to get expelled back to his country within a week. Although I made every effort not to do anything similar, I had problems due to my other activities. At work, we talked a lot about politics. I convinced some of my coworkers to follow me to the protests we organized to defend migrant rights. That bothered my bosses and I lost my job.

I had to look for another job at a time when the possibility of hiring migrants was suspended. Luckily, the country then known as Spain had a rapidly aging population. Its inhabitants hardly

108

ever had children, and there were countless old people without families. Jobs caring for the elderly were still available in special cases. I got one. Unfortunately, it wasn't easy. Almost all the old people used electric chairs and scooters to move around, even while they were accompanied by their respective carers. But I had to end up with the sheik who refused all the machines. He said his countrymen were made for spiritual matters, not to invent devices. Due to these ideas, I had to carry him on my shoulders when we went out to walk. The old man put on a cape he made himself out of old peseta bills, the former currency of that place, after he climbed on top of me. I raised his legs to my chest and he wrapped his thighs around my neck and his arms around my head. In this way, we took walks around the neighborhood; he met with old friends and they chatted while I held up his weight. They all lived in the suburbs and spoke in negative terms about the migrants who, as they said, had come to steal their pensions. When I spoke to them about the proletariat and class struggle, they hardly paid me any mind.

I didn't have much time to myself, since every day I had to take the old man out to walk, clinging on to my neck. I did so under ever sorrier conditions, all while noticing the repulsion in his eyes despite my great effort in holding him up.

One day some guards approached our group. I knew what they wanted, since I knew what migrant interrogation really meant after so many visits to the police station: the first step toward expulsion. It didn't matter that you didn't have a criminal record. They didn't judge me for my actions but for my place of birth, and for the skin color that gave away this origin. I tried to drop the old man and run away, but he clung on to me with such strength and squeezed my neck so hard he almost choked me. I lost consciousness; when I came to, the guards were already surrounding me. The whole time, the old man had not let go of me, he was still on my shoulders because the agents had kept us from falling over. They took us both to the police station and there, in the interrogation room, sitting on a chair with the old man on my shoulders, I had to answer a series of questions. I had to explain how I came to a country that had ceased to exist, to talk about my political activity and give the names of my friends. It should have been enough for the guards to hand me my expulsion order. From then on, the old man, who didn't get down from my neck anymore, not even to sleep, intensified his abuse, always threatening to turn me in if I put him down.

One day, I got sick of that deplorable situation and, with the damned sheik always on my shoulders, I headed to the wine shop on the plaza we frequented. I asked them to sell me a bottle of wine, which they wrapped up in a piece of paper so I could enjoy it in the street. I knocked it back. By the time we were crossing the plaza, I felt reanimated and happy; I started singing and dancing. The old man, realizing that my strength had been multiplied, ordered me to give him the bottle. I feared he would turn me in to the guards, and I didn't dare to tell him no. Grudgingly, I passed him the bottle. He took it in his hands, lifted it to his lips and drank to the last drop, then threw it far away. His companions goaded on the whole scene with chants and applause. Then he felt the effect of the wine on his brain. He started wobbling on my shoulders, holding himself up just barely enough so as not to fall. Then, noticing that he was no longer squeezing around me like usual, I unraveled his legs from my neck and, with a rapid movement, pushed him off me and threw him a few meters away from me. The old man fell badly; he didn't move. The other old men shouted at me. With the cell phones built into their electric scooters, they called the guard, who didn't take long to come after me even though I had already started my escape. The newly created "anti-immigrant shock forces" were obligated to fire only rubber bullets. Neverthe-

110

less, in my bad fortune, one of these bullets hit me right in the left eye, and I lost it. I also lost my residency in Europe because, at that instant, after arresting me, the guards accused me of abusing European citizens, put me on a plane, and sent me back to Songhai.

Even though I was well educated, I had done hard labor in the newly re-established European Union because, with the money I made, I provided my family with a higher income than if I were working in my own country in a position that corresponded to my degree. In Songhai, on the other hand, there was no work of any kind, much less after the massive wave of returning migrants expelled from Europe; at any rate, I couldn't stop fighting for my people's rights, and they don't like that in my country. I had to leave again because my life was in danger. Since then I have passed through many places, but I have always thought of returning to Europe.

After many days' journey, this very night I arrived in the city once known as Dorothea, where I met the one-eyed man who spoke before me. I told him I was a foreigner and he said the same thing. Then, by luck, fate guided us to you. And so we came to this blessed house. That is the reason for my empty eye and my shaved head.

After that story, it was the chosen one's turn, and he told his own tale, from the moment he left Shangana, from start to finish. It would be useless to repeat it here. When he finishes, he who speaks thinks that his is by far the best of the stories. But the young women do not feel the same way. They say it is the least interesting of the three. Who knows if this is because, out of them all, he is the only one who has never set foot in Europe. They throw him out on the street. The desire that washed over him before transforms into a hate that pushes him to carry on, to reach Europe and claim victory so he can return to Dorothea, to the damned house of the young women, but this time with enough money to possess them both.

The chosen one decides to put his coins to a different use from the one he first planned; he goes to the recruitment office for candidates for the pre-selection challenge of *Immigration: The Contest*, of which the first one-eyed man spoke. He comes across a low door into a house hidden in a little alleyway. He knocks. After a long wait, a man with milky skin appears in the threshold, skin lighter than that of the foreigners who wander the streets of the city known in the old days as Dorothea. He has a scornful look in his eyes and a deep scar on his right cheek. With him is an assistant with an oily complexion and cruel eyes. At first, the assistant treats him with disdain, but when he sees the bag of coins the chosen one has been hiding in his inner pocket until that moment, his attitude changes completely while his boss invites him to walk through the door.

Inside, in a dark room sparsely furnished with a table and a few chairs, along with many foreigners in the house's hallways, sleeping squeezed together on sheep skins, the chosen one and the contest's intermediaries close the deal. He hands over his coins. In exchange, they sign him up for the second challenge, which requires this procedure, and they give him a fake passport to get to his next destination. They do this after comparing the different images on their documents with the face and features of the chosen one. They try to find a face that looks like his, and one finally comes up. At that moment, he who speaks ceases to be himself. He becomes a fake person with a fake identity who moves across the borders of unknown, changing countries, while his double, the young man who appears in the image on the passport he says is his own, travels through some other place or perhaps lies eliminated far from the land where he grew up. The chosen one learns the name that appears on the passport—Mamadou—while he forgets his own. He knows he is losing his roots and this is a great sacrifice; then he thinks of his mother's amulet: if he cannot maintain his identity, may the first and last name that appear on a false document never be the sign of who he is, nor the epithet he will use later; may this sign be something that defines him unequivocally, even over the borders he must cross.

After sealing the deal, the chosen one must wait for several days in an abandoned house on the outskirts of the city known in the old days as Dorothea. There, the aspiring participants must remain in silence to show the intermediaries that they are ready and they are prudent. In the house, there is no more than a toilet and a little food. More than once, the chosen one thinks he has made a mistake, his adventure is coming to an end right there, he will end his days between the walls of the houses of the city known in the old days as Dorothea.

But one day, they knock on his door; at that moment he knows he must begin his journey. He sets off decisively down his path, along with a group of young men who gather beside the vehicle that will transport them, young men who walk out the doors of abandoned houses like his own.

At that moment, the drivers' boss, who is none other than the guy with milky skin, a scornful look in his eyes, and a deep scar on his face, tells them to get onto the transports. There are fifty young men on the vehicle watching the last rays of the sun while it moves toward the place where the dunes must end and dreams begin, dunes that seem endless and have not yet ended hours later, when the contestants discover that the organizers have decided to make the challenge harder: the intermediaries abandon them halfway through the journey, in the desert. They simply point out the path they must take, in the company of the skeletons of participants eliminated in previous seasons.

In these terrible conditions, the chosen one begins the challenge that, in the contest, they call classification, which Sub-Saharans must complete again and again in order to access the next phase, and which seems like it will never end, whether because of the distance from their countries to the sea that separates Africa from The Island of the Good Year or because those who were born south of the Sahara always seem to have something more to prove.

But the chosen one is not scared this time. He advances through the dunes more slowly every day, setting off into the three weeks of hell he must suffer in order to qualify. In their journey across the desert they barely have any water, forcing he who speaks to drink his own urine, trying to ignore the terrible smell. Some of his companions don't want to do this, and they fall eliminated in that inexorable hourglass. Nevertheless, the chosen one records the faces of each one who disappears in his memory. He shows proper respect to the remains of these comrades; and for each of them, he prays and builds a little monument to their memory in the desert. There is no other sense in carrying on alive among so many doomed to die, haughty young men just a few days before, sad bodies covered in sand at the end of their participation.

In the end, the chosen one looks out over the lights of the city once known as Melilla, the base of the contestant admission center, along with seven other companions. They head to the forest in the hills. Cissé had assured him that it was the best place to rest before the last challenge, the one that would let him access the final phase of the contest.

The forest is nothing but another challenge, one of resistance and survival during the constant raids that lead to direct elimination, which the chosen one must avoid, constructing a fake campsite to hide the real one. This is also a special place: the space where the chosen one becomes conscious of his nature, hand in hand with Frantz, a young man from Moka, once known as Equatorial Guinea, who speaks perfect Spanish and who, after confirming the physical capacity of he who speaks while fleeing from the guards, becomes convinced that he is the chosen one, the leader they need;

so he says. He assumes this to be true, although, more than Frantz's words, it is the memory of his eliminated companions and the crowd of people who suffer in order to classify that persuades him that someone must reach The Island of the Good Year, and that it might as well be him. From that moment on, he speaks of himself with that epithet.

Frantz encourages him to learn Spanish; he spends weeks teaching him. For this purpose, he tells him stories of the heroes of past migrations, using a very peculiar way of speaking, until he molds the chosen one's speech to the same tone. He also teaches him, this time along with his seven companions, how to build ladders and other tools for the final challenge, which Frantz has already tried to pass more than once, as is evidenced by his body covered in dents and bruises. Frantz also explains that they need gloves to get through the latest additions to the challenge. They spend a week looking for some in the bazaars of the city once known as Melilla. Finally, they choose the first pairs they find. Snow gloves in a place where it doesn't snow. When Frantz believes the chosen one is ready, he calls them together and they celebrate with a big dinner. They cut off the heads of fifteen chickens they had found among the waste of the local market one night, throw them in an old bucket, and make soup. They all eat together and then they pray, each to his own god. During the dinner, Frantz takes a little broth, mixes it with the liquor he hides for such occasions, and sprinkles them all with it. Then he drinks until the bottle is half empty. When he is finished, his eyes are murky. The chosen one believes he is overcome by some sort of strange possession. The other looks at him and says: Guide us, oh, you!, chosen one among the chosen. With you, victory is ours. But he also says something very strange. He advises him to stay away from water and warns him of the man who never ceases to be a child. He tells him that this man could be the obstacle that keeps him from achieving his

115

desires. The chosen one does not quite understand. He only recalls his deep fear of water. Then he remembers his eliminated companions and he squeezes his mother's talisman tight. He hopes it will help him get through the dangers of which Frantz has spoken. Then he drinks from the bottle of liquor to raise his spirits. After him, the others. They all follow Frantz, who points out the path. When they make out the fence that closes in the city, they can see the first light of dawn on the horizon.

After so many challenges, the chosen one is a consummate athlete. It is easy for him to dodge the mechanical dogs, but the same cannot be said for Frantz, who, thrown off by this new addition, succumbs and is eliminated by these robotic beings. But the chosen one must keep going. It is not hard for him to climb up the six meters that separate the highest part of the fence from the ground, and then to cross over the razor wire with little effort thanks to the snow gloves. He does so before the eyes of a young man with oily skin who reaches the highest part of the fence, but is not wearing gloves, and therefore does not pass the challenge. His companions suffer the same fate, even though they are well equipped. The exception is his friend Cissé, who he meets inside, which fills him with happiness, although he must warn him not to mention his old name.

Weeks later, he will cross paths with the young man with oily skin in the hallways of the contestant center, and that day he will find out that they call him the Kid. He must have cheated to get into the contest, since the chosen one saw how he failed to cross the fence. Then he remembers Frantz's words and thinks that perhaps this is the man who will never cease to be a child. That thought, and the hatred for queers he learned in Shangana, quickly lead him to join with Cissé and Amina. This happens when they eliminate the participants who complain about the hoses, and only four are left on The Island of the Good Year, from which the cho-

116

sen one must emerge, and that's him. Cissé is Amina's friend, he doesn't quite know why, but this leads them to start working together. Amina proposes that they do all they can to isolate the Kid. It's a good tactic, because he is at a disadvantage. Together, they bother him in every possible way. Especially Amina, who puts needles in the mattress on his bunk every night, as well as painting threatening messages on the communal wash basin after the chosen one teaches her to write in Spanish, not to mention the substances the young woman keeps in her locker.

One day, Cissé tells them he wants to go over to the French edition because he can express himself better in that language and he thinks he'll have better chances at winning. Then a young woman comes to take his place; it is a surprise for everyone. She gets on Amina's nerves from the first day, and she becomes a close friend of the Kid. From that moment on, he who speaks starts finding all of his underwear cut up in the worst place; they give the chosen one an image he doesn't like. He starts keeping guard over his clothes in the lockers. He doesn't know if it is the Kid's doing or the newcomer's; he finds no clues and this undermines his morale. Unsure of the environment he once controlled, the chosen one hears the Kid's first confessional during a special. He discovers it is full of negative messages against Africans; he realizes that the Kid has chosen the right words to win, the same words that Frantz forbid before setting out for the fence challenge. Then he understands that his condition as the chosen one is in danger. There can no longer be any doubt: the Kid is the man who will never cease to be a child, his worst enemy. He decides to confront him openly, to criticize all that he represents, especially because he does not earn many points with his confessional and he has to recover however he can. He gets through by showing himself to be the best participant in the physical challenges, and also thanks to the Kid's constant controversies in the specials. In arguments,

117

he always appeals to his strength, so that those who do not admire the Kid's culture might prefer his muscles by simple contrast. He imagines they are looking for muscle in these contests at any rate. In this way, he conceals his limitations in the guard challenge, which simply consists of trying to get past a police checkpoint, but it brings up the memory of the soldiers who occupy Shangana, and he refuses to throw the other participants to the other side of the fence when it's his turn, so his strength doesn't do much good. When the action is over, he doesn't feel like eating with the other contestants. The Kid falls sick that same night. The chosen one knows Ánima is to blame because, just after the special when the Kid spoke ill of Africans, he discovers Amina talking to her sister in the set's hallways. He who speaks hides so as not to be seen, by them or by the cameras; he hears how Ánima appeals to their family ties and to a debt contracted between them in the past, until Amina agrees to accompany her to the lockers, beside the communal wash basin, where she gives her a little flask that she selects from her formidable arsenal, which must have been the source of the poisoning. But the Kid survives because he's stronger than his slight figure lets on. Then comes the greenhouse challenge, which the chosen one wins along with Amina thanks to his ability to work under a scorching plastic sky, because he knows the Kid is still weak, which pushes him to exert himself even further. The hot bed challenge is another story, and at several moments he is almost overcome by sleep, even when he has to speak before the audience, which means that one day he must face Amina before the cameras, tired of her insistence that he convert to Islam since the day she took advantage of his fears during the first voyage. But he regains his composure and gathers up the strength to try to improve his Spanish, just as Frantz advised him. In this way he will become one of the favorites, even if learning the language spoken in the place he seeks to reach requires a great effort.

118

Nonetheless, now he is past all of this and he faces the final challenge, which he knows he will win since he has spent many weeks practicing, and because he is the chosen one and luck must smile on him in the end. ▉

When Mamadou's statement was complete, we threw over to the final episode's special guest. That was the night we chose the winner of every season. It's usually the program with our highest audience ratings. Sadly for everyone involved, the guest was none other than Silvio Pérez. He had publicly declared that he wanted to get involved in politics. Since he was of Spanish origin and it was his show, he concluded that a visit to The Island would be ideal. Pérez's participation in the special marked the start of his campaign run-up. I imagine he was thinking it might give him good results, as it did for the Minister. Bad idea.

After listening to the contestants, Pérez decided to confront each of them face to face before voting began. He did so in the most controversial way possible. He treated the Kid like an invalid, criticized Amina's hijab and fundamentalism, laughed at Mamadou's pretensions of grandeur, and made fun of Ánima's worldview, branding her a fake. His words raised the stir he was looking for, and we didn't have to wait long for accusations to start flying.

Maybe we did finally understand the truth of what happened on The Island, like the Kid's poisoning, through all the voices and all the superimposed versions of the events. But the truth always causes pain, and Pérez's words were the spark that lit the fuse of discord. Considering that the finalists believed their confessionals were only seen by the audience, not the rest of the contestants, the cries and disputes that erupted were no surprise. Mamadou wanted to punch the Kid over what he had done with his underwear; and, although the Kid laughed at his rival, he felt very hurt by Ánima's betrayal, which she didn't know how to hide from the camera. What nobody expected in the production team, and perhaps even less in the audience, was what happened next. Especially because, to avoid aggression among the participants, once the challenges were over we tried to make sure the set was aseptic, with hardly a single blunt object to be found. Nonetheless, in the midst of the uproar, Amina managed to take the floor. When we all supposed she was going to take the chance to launch into another of her anti-Western diatribes, when we thought she was going to verbally respond to Pérez, who had attacked her religious identity and attire, what she did was throw the wireless mic in a perfect arc that ended with a heavy impact on Silvio Pérez's mouth. He started bleeding copiously from his bottom lip in front of the cameras after spitting out a couple of teeth. The cloud of security guards who had accompanied him to the edge of the set had done no good. If what he wanted was an image that would fill the headlines of every news report in the newly re-established European Union, he got it. Nonetheless, I imagine he wasn't expecting to get what he wanted under such sorry conditions, because after a brief shot of his face we cut straight to a commercial break.

We crushed our audience records that day, but we also earned crushing indignation. Social media was burning with comments criticizing the scene and discrediting the contestants and the show. We had to call off the special, and also the voting. Public opinion started to question if it was fair to accept this sort of immigrants, who assaulted European citizens. Some said it wasn't right to walk into Europe and then slam the door behind you; others wondered why we were surprised, since we already knew how "the immigrants" acted. All the messages had the same tone. Even though we immediately, urgently disqualified Amina, the audience considered that none of the con-

122

testants in our edition that season had won the right to come in and form part of the Union's workforce because they hadn't worked hard enough nor had they respected the rules. They contacted us through all the various media the program uses to interact with its spectators. Popular opinion determined that we should come up with an extraordinary challenge or else the program didn't deserve a winner. That opinion, along with pressure from various political forces, was the true cause behind our designing a final challenge, not the lukewarm reasons published by the contest's directors.

At any rate, the most unexpected reaction came from the social democratic parties that, in an official statement signed by their leader, demanded the elimination of Amina and expressed support for the proposal of a special challenge, seconding popular demand. It was strange. The social parties were known among the production team for their constant criticism. They had decried human rights violations in all previous seasons of the contest. As always, this year they had protested during the hot bed challenge, considering it inhumane. It was a challenge that consisted of keeping one of the beds the temperature it would be if there were always a person sleeping in it. The contestants achieved this by taking turns lying in the same bed. It was a cooperative challenge. Every contestant had to endure not sleeping until it was time for their turn. With four participants, as we had in the Spanish-language sector, this means six hours of sleep a day, and the tiredness always provoked controversies and arguments. Of course, if they completed the challenge successfully, the program provided supplementary food, and the winners were allowed to sleep for a whole day in their own bed.

Without a doubt, the Kid did best at the challenge. His flexible body didn't need many hours of sleep; I suppose it was hardened on the streets on Tangiers. However, for the rest, it was a serious problem. We had to pause the competition halfway through because Mamadou fell asleep on the way to the confession booth and Ánima fainted

123

constantly. The relationships between contestants had deteriorated on The Island, as we could see in the argument between the two sisters, which we now know was only partially picked up by the cameras. So it was no surprise that they positioned themselves against the organization for humanitarian reasons.

This is why we were so surprised by the statement that Silvio Pérez received from the leader of the European social parties: Tony Schröder, who transitioned overnight from paternalism to a discourse of rights-for-responsibilities toward the contestants. That was strange for Pérez, who always made moves based on showmanship and business, and whose recent wounds had not changed his opinions in the least. It might be true that the elections on the horizon affected the events and that, after Pérez's incident, the social parties retook the initiative after a long time, trying to make political gains from the protective attitude that the Minister of Integration had always cultivated with Amina.

So, with very little time, we had to pull a final challenge out of our sleeves. The three finalists who remained in the contest had to build their own raft. Then they would have to navigate it from the crag where our edition took place to the "Eye of Europe," the islet where the communication tower that coordinated the monitoring of the Mediterranean had been constructed. The person who passed the challenge most comfortably, in the audience's judgment, would be considered the winner. But everything went wrong, including my attempt to help.

The challenge began with the process of building the canoe, which was carried out with African palms. The Kid and Mamadou dove into their work, cutting the trunks and preparing the wood, and Ánima's knowledge of technical design allowed them to build a boat sufficient for such a challenge. Faced with the risk of losing the prize altogether, it seemed that the contestants were willing to forget their quarrels and work together. For that reason, and to ease the pain of Amina's elimination, the production team provided the nails, screws, and other necessary metallic elements for the finalists. The idea was for the boat to be something more than the typical cayuco carved out of an empty log. I mediated with the production bosses to make the supplies happen. I was worried about my contestants' chances. Once again, my robot's soul and my interest in technology guided my steps. I thought the use of metallic structures would protect them. With the technical team, we confirmed that the boat could float, and this was corroborated by the drones that flew over the area. It seemed we could renew the contest's dynamic. I remember I felt proud of my support and the humble technology we provided while I saw them paddling at a strong pace toward the islet, at the start of the second phase of the challenge.

The problem came almost at the end, when the contestants could already make out the "Eye of Europe." I don't know if the technicians overexerted the antenna's power, if the boat's metallic pieces were not really in suitable conditions, or if the time estimate was faulty. All these causes have been put on the table after the fact. All we know for sure is that, in the middle of the challenge, we lost video signal. The control screens at the production center went black, silent. If I were a telecom technician, which I'm not, I'd say it was probably due to some problem with the electromagnetic waves emitted by the tower, and the closeness of the human beings; at least as far as the signal loss is concerned.

But nobody really knows what happened during that five minute lapse, without images, which was longer for the audience because we couldn't reconnect the transmission until much later to inform them of the events. The final free-access sequence was shot by a camera on one of the drones before it pulled away to recharge its batteries. It gave the impression that the contestants were well secured to the boat, although the waves were picking up, as the metallic supports provided by the production team, thanks to me, seemed to convincingly resist the pounding of the sea. Nonetheless, and everything I

125

say from now on is unknown to the audience because they were not able to see the images, when we recovered the signal the bolts, screws, and metallic parts had slipped out of the raft. They had been drawn towards the tower's magnetized antenna, where they remained, stuck. In particular, they had lost a metal reinforcement that the challenge's participants had incorporated into the hull to avoid leaks, which must have been what made the vessel flip over. At that moment, my heart flipped over too. Fate was working against me when I had the idea of convincing my bosses to provide those pieces in order to construct a more stable boat. The vessel had ended up in pieces, which wouldn't have happened if they had used another construction method. In the meantime, the waves had intensified and a coming storm was growing on the horizon. The contestants splashed through the choppy sea. I remember, at that moment, I was overcome by a profound sense of guilt, the same guilt that brought me to write this story. For a few seconds, all of my teenage anxieties returned. I wanted to be a robot again, an angelic Arale. To rectify the misfortune I had caused, as HAL 9000 hoped before being disconnected by David Bowman. To fly to the site of the accident with my robot powers and pull those unfortunate souls out of the water before dropping them off on dry land. And to do so with a smile on my lips and with the innocence of my childhood, so as not to watch those scenes without emotion, as I did four days ago.

At that instant we could see how the scrap of wood that kept Mamadou afloat was slipping out of his hands. Then we found out he didn't know how to swim. Nevertheless, the Kid, who was swimming gracefully with his slender body, and who only had two hundred meters left before reaching the craggy rocks on which the "Eye of Europe" was raised, decided to go back. He always said he was a good Muslim, although, given his history, we didn't believe him. In spite of the strong surges of the sea, he swam with astonishing power. He went back to try to pull the bully who, along with Amina, had made his life impossible for almost all of the contest out of the waters of the Mediterranean. From the production control room, we saw the Kid crashing through the water with all his might. We also saw Mamadou clinging desperately to his weak body. The Kid pushed with all his strength, only for them both to be dragged away behind a wave that appeared from out of nowhere and swallowed them up. We lost them from sight even as we called on the rescue teams. The stormy sea and the lightning that curiously struck the point of the "Eye of Europe" again and again made the rescue impossible. We could barely make out their arms one last time over the surface of the sea before they sank for good.

Only after a tense few moments did we recognize the bodies of Mamadou and the Kid again. They were in each other's arms, even after so many disputes and misunderstandings. Their lips were green and they were lying lifeless on the sandy beach of the islet of the "Eye of Europe," where the storm had abandoned them. They were shadows of a terrible fate that lay reflected on the wet sand of a beach across from the country formerly known as Libya, along with Mamadou's amulet, which lay on the dunes with a broken chain.

Before that, we had watched Ánima die. She had skillfully calculated the shortest route to the island, but she didn't realize she was leading them through an area riddled with reefs. A wave smashed her sullied body against the rocks, revealing that she would never lead a journey as epic as the one she had defended in her speech. Her impact against the reef coincided with Amina's scream and her fall, rolling down the stairs of The Island's set, the place where she asked to see the result of the final challenge even though she was already eliminated, taking advantage of the production team's internal transmission. To some extent, it was logical that she would be affected by her sister's death. It was clear that her idyllic image of The Island and her hopes for the future, at least for a peaceful future, had just been shattered.

After the storm, we had to recover and pile up the bodies, like the pain of past years piled up in an old man's wrinkles. We had to see

127

Ánima's disfigured face after her crash into the rocks and hours in the water; and the swollen bodies of Mamadou and the Kid. We had to bring those three unfortunate souls together on the sandy beach of The Island, where we put them in bags and then in white coffins sent from the newly re-established European Union. We had to make sure the smell of their rotting flesh didn't spread over the whole island.

The production team mobilized in its entirety before the authorities arrived; it didn't take them more than a day. There were the Minister of Integration, Silvio Pérez, Tony Schröder, and other leaders of the political bodies of the newly re-established European Union. All supposedly dispirited, as was seemingly evidenced in their speeches during the State funeral, and in the ceremony that ended with the burial of the three coffins in the center of The Island, televised on all the news channels. The Minister of Integration, who repeated that she had known the victims personally, was particularly heartbroken. I imagine she was thinking of the voters, as she seemed much more emotional than she had ever been on the contest's set.

Only later did we find out about the script of the special that Silvio Pérez wanted to re-air that night, with many censored scenes. Most of us refused to participate. Nevertheless, they soon brought over a technical team from the continent, which took our place, and that's why you've been able to see the images.

After that partial re-airing, the European audience has grown distressed. Their consternation began soon after the accident. Even my ex-girlfriend sent me a message in Spanish that she made public to the rest of her social media contacts in order to express her condolences the very night of the tragedy, after seeing what happened on the news. It said:

"sad about the bodies floating in the sea and the coffins on The Island. no justice! xxx"

That started a conversation that led me to call her on the phone and try to tell this story. It's curious to think about: in recent days, no one has remembered the crisis that led us to plan the final challenge. All the social buzz has concentrated on decrying the tragedy. I suppose that viral outpouring from the audience was what led the authorities, urgently convened with Silvio Pérez after the funerals, to make an unprecedented decision. For the first time in any of its editions since *Immigration: The Contest* began, an eliminated participant would immediately become the winner. In this case, what's more, she would become a European citizen. Amina has received special treatment. She has not been obliged to obtain an initial work permit, or to spend a number of years going through provisional integration after the fact, like previous winners. In a gesture of thanks, she apologized and was publicly rehabilitated in the tearful program broadcast by Silvio Pérez's production company four nights ago, when they contacted the Kid's family and Ánima and Amina's mother. It was impossible to locate Mamadou's family throughout the contest.

While she spoke to the camera, Amina carried herself with obvious affectation and more than a little restraint. She mentioned nothing of what she saw, which makes me think they rehabilitated her only in exchange for her silence. I still remember her setting off from The Island with all her belongings a few days ago. They had given her a sash that marked her as a new European citizen, but she still had that strange glint in her eyes that they had reflected throughout the season. This time, she was not accompanied by any politician. They had all abandoned the set. I'm the only one left in the production control room, now deserted. Here, I have recorded what I think is the true story of *Immigration: The Contest*. The text I now complete in this virtual space, open to the world. But I can already see the morning on the horizon, and I should keep quiet, discrete. ⊞

THANKS

★★★★★★★★★★★★

To my wife and son for their emotional support throughout the writing process.

To Gema Pérez-Sánchez, without whose guidance this book would have been impossible.

To Mariana González and the Tot Raval association for giving me the necessary contacts to interview migrant associations in the Raval district of Barcelona.

To Conchi Fernández Zapata for putting me in touch with the Escola d'Adults of La Llagosta

To Huma Jamshed, president of ACESOP, and to Javed Ilyas, president of the Associació de Treballadors Pakistanesos.

To Abdul and Mohamed for their help and hospitality in our interviews.

To the Programa de Salvamento Marítimo of the Red Cross in Andalucia for their willingness to answer my questions.

To my friends and partners: Bárbara Serrano, Hernán Francese, Maribel Ruiz, Roberto Ramírez, Omar Villasana, Jorge Morales, Matías Crowder, Boris Lazzarini, and Israel Paredes for their suggestions and corrections.

An advanced reader will have recognized literal quotes from Juan Goytisolo, Hannah Arendt, Italo Calvino, and the multiple authors who wrote the *One Thousand and One Nights*. I also give my thanks to them.

Immigration: The Contest
Bad News from The Island

Carlos Gámez Pérez
Translated by Arthur M. Dixon